Two friends discover they aren't backward...they're just late bloomers.

EMILY JONES: I feel like a hothouse tomato somebody stuffed in the ground, then forgot to water. I think I'm doing fine—until I look down at my shoes. *Good lord.* One blue and one black. That's what I get for trying to be the kind of widow who glides gracefully through grief instead of what I am—a slightly hysterical woman who doesn't have the foggiest idea of how I'll get through the rest of my life.

DELTA JORDAN: I used to see myself as unencumbered and free. These days I feel like a woman who has gone through life missing out on the best things, like someone to hold my hand and let me tuck my cold feet against his warm legs. And when I'm with Antonio, he's not like any other man I've known. He's a talented, disarming man with warm hands that hold mine and make me feel like a woman set free.

Peggy Webb

Peggy Webb and her two chocolate Labs live in a hundred-year-old house not far from the farm where she grew up. "A farm is a wonderful place for dreaming," she says. "I used to sit in the hayloft and dream of being a writer." Now, with two grown children and more than forty-five romance novels to her credit, the former English teacher confesses she's still a hopeless romantic and loves to create the happy endings her readers love so well.

When she isn't writing, she can be found at her piano playing blues and jazz or in one of her gardens planting flowers. A believer in the idea that a person should never stand still, Peggy recently taught herself carpentry.

PEGGY WEBB

Late Bloomers

LATE BLOOMERS

copyright © 2007 by Peggy Webb

isbn-13:978-0-373-88128-4

isbn-10:   0-373-88128-2

TheNextNovel.com

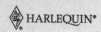 HARLEQUIN®

PRINTED IN U.S.A.

From the Author

Dear Reader,

I could pretend all my books are pure fiction, but fans of *Driving Me Crazy*, *Flying Lessons* and *Confessions of a Not-So-Dead Libido* would march to Mississippi and switch me with a magnolia branch. By now you know that I tap heavily into my own experiences to find my Harlequin NEXT novels.

Late Bloomers grew out of the months I spent with my cousin Shirley when we discovered that laughter is really the best medicine. Her lively spirit permeates this book. So does her kamikaze driving of her big RV. That I lived to tell this tale is a miracle!

And how did Italy end up in a book about two Southern women discovering themselves? Years ago I studied screenwriting in Assisi, and since that time the magic of Italy has bloomed in my soul. I'm delighted to share the magic with you.

Enjoy this zany, poignant ride with Emily and Delta. Then visit my Web site to let me know what you think— www.peggywebb.com. Be sure to enter the *Late Bloomers* contest. I'm having beautiful, embroidered book bags designed especially for you!

Happy reading!

Peggy

P. S. The Project Linus mentioned in this book is a wonderful, nonprofit volunteer organization "providing security through blankets." To find out more visit their Web site at www.projectlinus.org.

To my sisters, Jo Ann and Sandra, for love, laughter and support, and to my magical unicorn for inspiration.

CHAPTER 1

When you're traveling to a foreign country for an extended period, it's best to learn the language.

The Seasoned Traveler's Guide to Tuscany,
Delta Jordan

Emily

I feel like a hothouse tomato somebody jerked out of the pot and stuffed in the ground, then forgot to water.

I thought I was doing fine, all dressed up, finally back on the piano bench at Smithville Baptist Church playing the prelude.

Then Laura McCord, the town's failed opera singer and chief busybody, leaned over and said, "Pssst, Emily. Your shoes."

Good lord. One blue and one black.

That's what I get for trying to be a Nancy Reagan kind of widow who glides gracefully through grief instead of what I am—a slightly hysterical, totally clueless, recently bereaved woman who doesn't have the foggiest idea how I'll get through the rest of my life without Mike Jones.

I don't think I should get out of the house again for about six years. Why didn't I take Delta's advice? She's smarter than I am, more educated, more beautiful, more *everything*. If she weren't my first cousin and best friend, I'd hate her.

"Emily, you've got to let yourself grieve. Hole up and just let it rip. Stop prancing around trying to act like Bob Hope entertaining the troops."

That's me to a T, always front and center, making sure everybody is having a good time, spinning tales, making them laugh. Even in the aftermath of death, for Pete's sake.

Delta writes travel guides at the speed of light— a workaholic, her husbands said—and I finally convinced her to go on to Hot Springs where she's researching not one but two guides—one to spas and the other to great Southern restaurants.

Although I'm three years older, it has always seemed the reverse to me. She came into this world screeching and batting her fists against the injustice of being jerked out of the safe haven of the womb into a remorseless world where her daddy would vanish under cover of night when she was six, and both her husbands would walk out to "find something more"—as if there were anything in this world better than Delta Jordan.

I'd hugged her hard, and then said, "You go on now, Delta. It's high time for me to grow up."

She knew exactly what I meant. Mike petted and pampered me and protected me from life's messy chores, such as balancing checkbooks. If I'm to survive without him, I've got to start learning how to do a few things by myself.

But first I have to finish playing the prelude. I don't know what possessed me to think I could sit here only three months after the funeral praising the Lord with music instead of wanting to box his Holy jaws for prematurely jerking my husband up to Glory Land.

Granted, Mike was sixty-five, fourteen years older than I. Still, he had the joie de vivre of a forty-year-old. What he didn't have was the capacity to win over the cancer cells that invaded his brain.

I'm going to beat this thing," he'd say, even after all his hair was gone and he could barely put his harmonica to his lips. I believed him. I would picture the Big C slinking off in the face of Mike's rip-roaring rendition of "Mess Around."

He loved blues. It's the kind of music you fall into, the kind that leaves no room for death and the injustice of being the one left behind to cope.

"Pssst, Emily." Laura McCord taps me on the shoulder again. "Stop it."

I drown her out, falling into this music, tapping the rhythm with my fashion faux pas shoes. The preacher gets down from his pulpit and heads my way.

"Emily, I'll have somebody take you home. I don't believe this church is ready for rockabilly."

To my mortification I realize I've segued from high church music to Ray Charles's "Mess Around."

Maybe I am losing my mind and I'm only imagining myself a widow. Maybe Mike is holed up somewhere right now consulting with the best psychiatrists about my care.

I stand up, unable to look at anybody, unable even to remember where I parked my car. Mercifully, somebody takes my arm and leads me from the church.

"I'll drive you home in your car. Laura can pick me up after church."

The voice brings him into focus, Mike's fishing buddy and Laura's husband, good old salt-of-the-earth Jim McCord, who has endured her warbling and gossip for fifty years. They make crowns for people like him.

When we get home, eagles are flying along the Tenn/Tom Waterway that meanders behind my house. I feel the power and pull of wings, as if Mike flew off somewhere wonderful and I am left earth-bound and longing.

"Do you want to lie down?" Jim asks.

What I want to do is sit on the deck awhile. Three years ago, when we finally decided to sell our too-big, empty-nest home near Tupelo's Country Club and move thirty miles to this rustic, multilevel house featuring a bank of windows facing the water, Mike fell in love with the eagles, and so did I.

Now, mesmerized by their graceful, arcing flight and the blue of water and sky melting together in the too-warm temperatures of an unusually hot Mississippi spring, I stand on my deck imagining myself flying off with them.

The eagles circle low, then light on their aerie atop a bald cypress in the shallows of the river. This is a sight too beautiful not to share, but when I turn to point this out to Mike, Jim's the one standing on the deck.

His bald spot is turning red with anxiety, thick glasses are sliding down his sweat-slick nose and his large, liver-spotted hands look like small beagle puppies. Suddenly I feel a rush of comfort. The sight of him in that exact spot is so familiar I expect to see his fishing gear and his old canvas fishing hat resting on the redwood decking behind him. I'll ask him—as I have a thousand times—how many catfish he and Mike caught, and then I'll laugh because Mike is always the one who stays at the boat to clean the fish.

Any minute now my husband will come whistling up from the waterway, his Mississippi State baseball cap battered and droopy from too many accidental dunkings in the river.

"Emily, are you all right?" Jim asks. "Can I get you anything?"

Get my husband, and make it snappy. That's what I want to tell him. *Go down to the boat and tell Mike to quit messing around and get his cute butt home. The joke's over. I don't want to play widow anymore. Let's play something else. Dominoes or Chinese checkers.*

"Maybe you ought to lie down. I can get you an aspirin."

Just what the doctor ordered. Take two aspirin and wait for everything to be normal again.

"How about some pie?" I say.

"You want some pie?"

"Oh, goodness, no. Come in, Jim. I'll make coffee and we'll have pie. Lemon icebox. One of Laura's."

Her saving grace is that she takes pies to the sick and afflicted, but I stuck every one of them in the freezer so I wouldn't have to think of my husband that way, which just goes to show the state I'm in. Denial.

I stride through the door, safe in familiar territory now. I know how to do this. I know about dinners for twelve and linen napkins and eggshell china and cucumber sandwiches served on white bread with the crusts cut off.

Maybe I'll throw a big house party, invite everybody I know, tell them to bring their sleeping bags and stay awhile. Two or three years. Maybe five. Long enough for me to get used to this awful realization: I'm in a foreign country called Grief and I don't have the faintest idea how to speak the language.

After Jim leaves, I shower and put on my favorite fuzzy blue robe, although it's only the early part of the afternoon. I'll sleep in it, then wear it all day tomorrow. It saves making decisions. They all seem so big now.

Emerging from my bathroom I hear the recorded message on my answering machine: "Hello. You've reached Mike and Emily Jones. We're not home right now, but please leave a message."

Well, he's half right. Emily's here, but Mike's not. Maybe that's him calling to say he'll be late driving back from wherever he is—Texas, to advise his bossy sister Lucille about the family ranch—and I should save him some pie.

But no, it's Delta.

"Emily, are you there? Pick up."

I grab the phone as if it's my lifeline. Which it is.

"I'm here," I say, and then I start bawling. Delta is the only person besides Mike I've allowed to see every one of my feelings and emotions, no matter how messy or ridiculous.

When my cat Leo became the victim of a hit-and-run because I was too busy being a newlywed to see him streaking through the open door, Mike got a new kitten for me. But Delta came over with a six-pack of Hershey's bars with almonds, two white candles for an all-night vigil and a book called *Cat Hymns* for the memorial service.

"Em, I'm coming right home, and don't try to stop me."

Both her husbands accused her of being bossy and arrogant. But, in spite of the fact that she speaks four languages and has three degrees, Delta clings to the ludicrous belief that somehow she was at fault for the cowardly desertion of two knuckleheads not worthy to tie the laces of her pink high-top running shoes.

Anybody looking at the two of us—me, short and dumpling-shaped with graying blond, curly Brillo-pad hair and Delta, tall and willowy with lush lips and an abundant fall of rich red hair—would guess that she was the one who knows everything about love but nothing about taking care of herself instead of exactly the opposite.

"Delta Jordan, if you come home I'm going to whip your butt. Good grief. All that traveling you have to do. Arkansas and Alabama then *Italy*, for goodness' sake!"

"You can go with me. A change of scenery would be good for you."

"Forget it. I'd as soon eat arsenic as get on a plane."

After we say goodbye, I curl up on my end of the sofa with the rest of the lemon icebox pie and a big spoon. The spot where Mike always sat looms so large, I take six bites without putting the spoon down. Leo the Fourth, an overweight Persian, jumps into my lap and starts purring.

I think cats know. I think they read minds.

Normally Leo switches around the house as if he owns it and merely tolerates my presence. But since Mike has been gone, Leo has turned into a one-cat comfort machine, all soft fur and warm weight and soothing noises.

I finish the pie then set the dish on the floor, something I would never have done in my other life—my life as the luckiest woman in the universe married to a man I was going to grow old with and love till we both keeled over holding hands. Our last words to each other would be *I adore you. Always and forever.*

Furious that I was deprived of that dream, I flip through the channels, avoiding Mike's favorites, the ones featuring baseball and hard-nosed detectives and ancient history.

Death is not a three-handkerchief movie: it's a thief that sneaks up on you and steals the beautiful goodbyes. I was in the kitchen chipping ice to spoon over Mike's cracked lips when he died. The last words he said to me were, *I'm thirsty.* The last I said to him were, *Hold on, darling. I'll be right back.*

I did go right back, but it was too late.

Leo revs up his motor while I stare at the menu channel, dry-eyed and droopy. My bed now seems as vast and frightening as the storm-tossed Pacific. I don't want to go back there. If I get a long telephone cord, I can sit on my end of the sofa the rest of my life ordering Chinese takeout.

I jerk awake at the loud crash on my deck, certain I'm going to be attacked by a band of cutthroats, murdered while I sit groggy-eyed on the end of my sofa with a crick in my neck. Leo arches up from my lap, hissing and spitting, confirming my suspicion that intruders intend to steal my cash then torture me till I sign over the fortune Mike left in two Tupelo banks, as well as the deeds to all his properties.

"Not without a fight, you don't."

I creak upward, hang onto the sofa till I get my running legs, then race down the hall to the bedroom closet and grab Mike's twelve-gauge, double-barreled shotgun.

I've read about things like this. Thieves comb the newspapers, reading the obituaries so they can prey on unsuspecting, unprepared widows.

Do I have a surprise for them! Mike taught me how to use this thing. If I can knock a Campbell's soup can off a cedar fence post, I can certainly burn the air close enough to reform a thief.

Leo's still hissing as I round the corner with vengeance and reformation on my mind. But the pie plate on the floor ambushes me, and I go down in a heap, the blast of the shotgun rendering me helpless and temporarily deaf.

When my ears stop ringing and I finally get off the floor and turn on the lights, I see an overturned bird feeder and the prehensile tail of a fat-butted opossum retreating from the deck. I also see the star-strung Milky Way and a silver crescent moon shining through the new hole in my roof.

I could cry about the hole or be thankful the intruder was an opossum or dial 911 and ask for help. Instead I lie on my back on the carpet and stare at the sudden starlight pouring into my living room.

For one brief, sweet moment I feel as if Mike has reached down and brushed his hand against my cheek.

CHAPTER 2

Although there are many claims surrounding the effervescent waters of the world's best spas, tales of miraculous emotional healings are unfounded. The best medicine for a wounded spirit is a good friend.

The Seasoned Traveler's Guide to Spas,
Delta Jordan

Delta

Evening is the part of my day I dread most, the hushed, expectant hours when work is done, morning seems a millennia away and there's nothing to fill the void except books or music or television or late night snacks—for one.

I used to calculate the odds of finding someone

who would share my evenings. When the odds went down to sixty-to-one, I quit.

Some women are destined to have only one place setting on the table and one pillow on the bed. I got suspicious I might be one of those when my first husband, Steve Jackson, rode off on his Harley-Davidson after a three-month trial run at marriage. When Larry (Mr. Wright, who turned out to be Mr. Wrong) ambled back to Oklahoma after only six weeks, I figured out that I'm at the top of the list.

The compensation is that you get to hang the toilet paper any way you like and you get the whole closet to yourself. Just spread out and hog the entire space. Be messy. Toss your shoes every which way. Nobody's there to complain.

I try not to think about my relationships or the lack thereof. I breathe deeply and carry on. No vague regrets. No nebulous hopes. Just put one foot in front of the other and try to pay attention. That's all. Sit up and take notice of the world. Pick a daffodil. Bend to pet a dog. Help an old man across the street. Eat ice cream and be grateful.

I organize my day's research notes, prepare my

agenda for tomorrow, watch the ten o'clock news, slather on night cream and then sit in the middle of the hotel's ubiquitous beige carpet and do yoga.

When my cell phone rings and Buddy Earl Lumpkin's cell phone number pops up, I consider not answering. Since I met him at Emily's Christmas party four years ago, he has been my most ardent suitor, popping over every time I visit her and calling with the regularity of a telemarketer. Actually, he's my only suitor in more years than I care to remember. If I wanted to spend the rest of my life being worshipped by Howdy Doody in plaid golfing shorts and a cowboy hat, he'd be the ticket.

But he's also Emily's neighbor, and because her children and her sister-in-law live so far away, I'm Em's emergency contact. I must answer.

I say hello, and Buddy Earl tells me Emily blew a hole in her roof.

"Is she all right?" I ask.

"I guess so. As soon as I heard the shotgun blast I ran right over. She was just lying in the middle of the floor smiling."

"Where is she now? Can I speak to her?" When

Emily comes on, I say, "I'm coming home. I'll leave first thing tomorrow."

"Buddy Earl said he could fix the roof."

"Don't argue. I'm coming anyway."

After I hang up, I start packing. This is not about repairing the roof. This is about patching a heart and shoring up a spirit. This is about being the safety net for your best friend until her broken wings grow strong enough to fly again.

Emily

I had expected Delta to arrive with her computer, a briefcase full of notes and the suitcase she took to Hot Springs, Arkansas. Instead, she gave up the lease to her apartment in Tupelo, packed her red Jeep Liberty Sport and arrived yesterday afternoon with all her personal possessions.

"I'm moving in for a while," she announced.

It's like having God move in, somebody who knows everything, does everything right and makes you glad to be trailing along in the tailwinds.

I heard her up this morning at six leaving for her

run. Now I'm in my kitchen with my eyes barely open and she's back wearing a sweaty T-shirt with a slogan that proclaims, Well-behaved Women Rarely Make History. She has another that says, Good Girls Go To Heaven, Bad Girls Go Everywhere.

This is a quirky Delta only I know. She's a perfect lady in public, but when she feels safe enough to let her guard down—which is rarely—she shows this wicked, bawdy side that reinforces my belief that her two husbands were underendowed, moronic troglodytes.

"Get dressed," she says. "We're going to take Mike's rowboat out so I can get an upper-body workout, then we're going to drive to Mooreville and check out that little restaurant that serves country ham and redeye gravy."

"I've made breakfast and I am dressed and I don't want to go anywhere."

"The restaurant is for research and you're wearing your robe and you're going."

She leads me down the hall, rummages in the tangled jungle of my closet, pulls out shorts and a T-shirt, while I just float along behind her. Grateful.

When we go outside, Buddy Earl nearly falls off the roof gawking at her.

"Hey, Delta," he yells. "Want to come over to my house tonight and watch wrestling? I could give you the thrill of a lifetime."

"No thanks, Buddy Earl. If my life gets any more thrilling, I won't be able to stand the excitement."

While Delta's dragging Mike's boat closer to the dock I say, "Maybe you should go out with Buddy Earl. At least you'd be doing something besides babysitting me. Who knows? You might meet somebody interesting if you'd get out and play."

"Shut up and row, Em."

Mike always said I rowed backward. Maybe I do everything backward—get married, have kids, become a widow, then finally grow up and learn how to take care of myself.

Instead of calling myself backward, perhaps I'll just say I'm a late bloomer. The trouble is, when am I going to bloom?

We row across the waterway and drop anchor in the shade of the heavy tree line on the other side where the eagles nest.

Mike's presence is strong here, almost as if I could reach out and touch him, talk to him, ask him how he's doing. But the thing I want to ask most is, Why in the world didn't you let me do a darned thing, and what am I going to do about your real estate business when I can't even keep my household bills straight?

Instead, I ask Delta.

"Tomorrow you're going with me to check out the barbecue at Little Dooey's in Columbus, and when we get home I'm going to walk you through Mike's account books then sit back and watch you bloom," Delta says.

"You just want me to eat the barbecue because you have to take antacid tablets." Delta gives me this look. "All right. I'll go to Columbus, but don't even think about me going to Italy."

"Italy's beautiful. You're going to love it."

"You know darned good and well I'm scared to fly. I can't do *everything* just because you think I'm pitiful and it will be good for me."

"Look on the bright side, Emily. You could have

acid reflux and Howdy Doody. Now, let's get this boat to the shore and check out the redeye gravy. I have work to do."

See, I think that's Delta's main problem: she's *always* working and never taking a single minute to do something fun unless it's for somebody else.

And besides, she never did deny that she thinks of me as pitiful.

Delta's mad at me because I'm in my robe again and my cat peed on her shoes, and I'm mad at myself because I didn't catch on too well when she was explaining Mike's books. I lied and told her I did so she'd quit worrying about me. She has a deadline to meet.

Now I'm on the phone lying to Lucille.

She thinks there's a timetable for grief. Month one, cry. Month two, clean out the deceased's closet. Month three, become a business whiz even though you can't balance your checkbook.

I think month one ought to be extended for about a year or two, and I don't think blow a hole in the roof is even on the list.

"Don't you worry about a thing, Lucille. I have everything covered, including Mike's business affairs."

What a joke!

"Are you sure about that, Emily?" Lucille says. "I could come up and show you the ropes. The ranch can spare me for a month or two."

Good Lord. There'd be murder on the Tenn/Tom. I'd go to Italy before I'd put up with Lucille.

"There's no need, Lucille. Brennan and Michele would come at the drop of a hat if I needed them."

That's no lie. My children would already be here if they knew the shape I'm in. But when they call I tell them I'm okay. There's no point in Brennan leaving his wife and sons, let alone his criminal law practice in Florida, and Michele leaving her husband and medical practice in Alabama, just to babysit me. You do these things for your children— pretend you're brave when you're not.

Now I say to Lucille, "Besides, Delta is here."

Delta's the only person I know who can outmaneuver, outwit and outrage my sister-in-law. The mention of her name is enough to send Lucille scuttling backward.

"Well, in that case I've got to go. I have the Double Bar J to run, you know."

I hang up while Mike's account books stare at me from accusing piles. Maybe if I eat something good it will improve my concentration. Maybe if I take them with me I'll absorb some business savvy by proximity.

Delta

As I type *The End*, Buddy Earl's hammer finally stops. He could have built Rome in the time it took him to repair that hole.

I open my e-mail, send the finished guide on spas to my editor, then walk upstairs to see how Emily's doing with the books.

Good Lord, the kitchen looks like the aftermath of an elephant stampede. Every casserole known to man lines the kitchen cabinets, Emily's tacky robe has vanished under an array of icings and Buddy Earl's standing there leering at me. I want to put a sack over my head and run.

While Emily writes his check for the roof repair,

he winks at me. Some women get lobster with butter while I get a Moon Pie with RC Cola.

Buddy Earl finally leaves and Emily stares at the mess she's made through bleary, mascara-streaked eyes.

"I don't know what to do," she wails. "Somebody ought to write a guide for widows. Something that tells you what to do next."

I hand her a paper towel and she blows her nose.

"You do it, Delta. You're good at knowing the right thing to do."

What I'm good at is running. What I'm good at is burying myself so deep in work I don't have time for a real life that involves relationships with people who are going to leave you in the end.

The really bad thing about being left by a daddy and two husbands is that I never saw it coming. Not once. I thought Daddy and I would spend the rest of our summers watching baseball and fishing. I thought he would attend my graduation, give me away at the altar and teach my children to love the outdoors the same way he taught me.

One night I went to sleep secure, and the next morning I woke up abandoned.

Even worse, people do something wonderful to make you think they'll be there forever—like take a six-year-old to a baseball game and buy hot dogs plus ice cream—then they vanish in the night.

My first husband was a musician, born with a steel guitar attached to his umbilical cord and wanderlust in his blood. But I traveled, too, and always came home, always wanted to come home.

We both got back from road trips at the same time. There were two suitcases on the bed, but only one person unpacking.

And Larry…my Lord, that man had the charm of a snake oil salesman. He'd flitted from one job to the next, always using his silver tongue. When he landed in my lap I bought into his big dream of someday owning a big country store where he'd sell everything from mule halters to wedding gowns, a sort of a country man's Wal-Mart.

Neither of my husbands said, I'm having problems, let's see if we can work things out. They just tossed the problem (me) aside and left to find something better.

After Daddy left, Mother was too busy paying the rent and putting food on the table to worry about taking a little girl out to have fun or shaping her future. What I learned about familial love came from time spent at Emily's house and hours reading *Little House on the Prairie*. I was a college senior when Mother died of a heart attack, and it was more like losing a ghost than a member of the family.

If Emily needs help piecing a quilt or picking the latest crop of apples, I'm the resident expert. Anything she wants to know that can be learned from a book, I'm the one to ask.

But I'm the wrong woman for advice about matters of the heart. I'm a woman without connections, a woman who can fit her prized personal possessions into three suitcases and still have room for an umbrella and a plug-in coffeepot.

I'm a fraud. I just hope she doesn't catch on.

I put my arms around her and just hold on. For both our sakes, I think.

"Tomorrow morning we're going to Mike's CPA

and let him help you hire a business manager. Then we're driving to City Grocery in Oxford to check out their shrimp with cheese grits. And after that, I have to do my Alabama research."

And then, *hallelujah*, Italy. I was never happier than when I was there doing my guide to Tuscany. I was twenty-two and still believed in the possibilities of love.

"Okay." Emily blows her nose again. "The CPA and Oxford work for me. But you can forget about Italy. You couldn't hog-tie me and drag me there."

My Lord, is she reading my mind?

It's not trying to get Em to Italy that I'm worried about. It's Hoover, Alabama, and the hornet's nest of memories waiting for me there.

Emily

After my kitchen debacle yesterday I have to do something to prove that I can stand on my own two feet, so I tell Delta I can talk to Mike's CPA all by myself, then I get in the silver Lexus and start down the road—not even wearing my blue robe.

I feel like a woman who can organize Vardaman, Mississippi's Sweet Potato Queen Contest and still have enough energy left to put together their Sweet Potato Festival. Just not like a woman willing to risk life and limb flying to Italy. My Lord, I'm scared to be on a six-foot ladder, let alone an airplane.

The only thing I dread about today is facing John Tedford's receptionist.

She always sports a tanning-bed glow, wears the latest designer fashions, size two, and makes me feel underdressed and uneducated. She actually used to move the *Fortune* magazines out of my reach when I accompanied Mike and hand me the *Ladies' Home Journal*.

But the worst part was when she took my purse.

"Here, let me put it in a safe place so you won't forget it," she'd say.

There ought to be a law against women like her. Once, in one of those stupid moments you wish you could take back, I accused Mike of making eyes at her. My exact words. *Making eyes*.

He just looked at me in that way he has. *Had*. That look that said, *How can you doubt my love?*

But I was up the proverbial creek and didn't know how to find the paddles, so I said, "Do you wish I looked more like Barbara? Do you wish I weighed fifty-five pounds instead of a hundred and fifty-five?"

"Darling, Barbara looks like a burnt toothpick. When I make love to you I know I'm in bed with a real woman."

This memory is so vivid I have to spend five minutes in my parked car getting myself under control. Of course, part of my dalliance could be fear. Even though I'm wearing a nice denim skirt and a presentable white blouse, I dread facing the perfect Barbara.

Finally I dab my eyes, powder my nose and get out of the car. But I hang onto my purse. She'll get it today only over my dead body.

"Good morning," she says when I walk in. "Do you have an appointment?"

See. She thinks I don't have the brain of a gnat.

"I most certainly do."

She checks the appointment book, her perfectly made-up face marred by a little frown wrinkle between her eyes. If she keeps that up, it will become permanent in about ten years.

Finally she says, "You can go in. Oh, do you want me to put your purse in safekeeping so you won't forget it?"

"No, thank you. My mind is a steel trap."

John is waiting for me, dwarfed behind his big mahogany desk. He has always put me in mind of Dopey, the sweet little dwarf with the droopy ears and the not-so-big brain. In fact, John is a member of Mensa. That just goes to show, you never can judge a person by his looks.

For which I am eternally grateful. Otherwise Mike would never have given me a second glance, never would have slid into the seat beside me at Logan where I waited to pick up a college friend, would never have asked about the book I was reading. *The Tao of Physics*, of all things. One of Delta's books that she had urged on me; I couldn't understand a single page, even after reading each one three times. Still…

"Emily. How nice to see you."

John gets up, takes my elbow and leads me to a maroon leather wingback chair beside huge bay windows. I love this view of Tupelo, the copper spire of the hundred-year-old courthouse rising in the distance, the big magnolia trees getting ready to burst into bloom, the graceful old Victorian house next door, restored and painted yellow with green shutters, the shingle out front in old English lettering, Jim Beale, Attorney at Law.

John sits in a chair beside me. "How're you doing, Emily?"

He's just punched a hole in that big reservoir of tears I carry around, and I feel them leaking from the corners of my eyes and sliding down my cheeks. John gets up and hands me a box of tissues from the corner of his desk.

"Well..." I clear my throat. "I'm well. Really. This is not a social call, John."

I tell him the job I want him to do, then thank him for handling the day-to-day details of Mike's real estate business in the interim.

"He was more than a client, he was a friend." John locks his hands and makes a steeple of his fingers. "Now, tell me exactly what you're looking for."

"Oh, well. About six feet tall, olive skin, wire-rimmed glasses, dark, dark hair." I see Mike striding toward me through Logan Airport. Then I see him waving from the edge of the waterway. "Maybe turning a little gray at the temples. Oh, and his hands…they're just beautiful."

John's giving me funny looks, so I try very hard to make him understand what I want.

"I don't know how to explain what the sight of those hands does to me. They are perfectly formed with curving thumbs."

"Emily…"

"I melt at the sight of them."

I'm melting now. All over. Nose. Eyes. Mouth. Tears everywhere. I'm Hoover Dam, unleashed.

John gets up and hugs me and I lean into him, grateful. His skinny shoulder acts like a sandbag plugging the leak, and finally the flow becomes a trickle.

"I know how hard it must be. Look, why don't you go home, get some rest? Meantime, I'll go ahead and find somebody and when you're up to it, we'll all talk."

"Okay." I stand up on legs that belong to a rubber chicken, then wobble my way toward the door.

"Emily. You forgot your purse."

"I was just coming back to get it. Thank you, John."

I sneak down the hall to the bathroom and fix my face before I leave. I don't want Barbara to see me this way.

In fact, I put an extra priss in my step when I walk by her desk.

"How did it go, Emily?"

"Great. Just fabulous. Fortune 500 is probably going to call me tomorrow for advice."

I don't know how long I hide in my car. With the windows rolled up and the motor off, I'm going to suffocate. Grieving Widow Found Dead, the headlines will say, then Michele and Brennan will spread my ashes on the Tenn/Tom exactly the way I've instructed. But first they'll follow the edict that made them roll their eyes and made Mike laugh.

"I want you to spray my ashes with Jungle Gardenia first. I want to go back to this earth smelling good."

It was Mike's favorite fragrance, and I know that's how he'll find me in the afterlife. By that heady, sensual scent.

I take big gulps of air, then turn the key in the ignition and hold my face in front of the air-conditioning vent. I don't want to be cremated and spritzed with Jungle Gardenia just yet.

I'll want to return home with strawberries then make a pie. For Delta. Something's bugging her about her guide to restaurants, but she won't tell me because I'm a basket case who thought John's office was an airport.

I drive to Kroger's and the produce section waylays me. California Grown, the label on these strawberries proclaims.

Mike and I went there on our honeymoon. Anaheim. Disneyland, because I'd always wanted to go, and he said everybody ought to have a chance to wear hats with mouse ears and shake hands with Mickey himself.

I tear myself loose, then roll my cart toward checkout where the girl behind the counter stares at me as if I've grown a third eye and sprouted rabbit ears.

"Looks like you cleaned us out," she says. "Are you sure you want all these?"

"Of course." Doesn't everybody need twenty-five cartons of strawberries for one pie?

I wonder if she's kin to Barbara. I wonder if she's

getting ready to call somebody to come and haul me off in a tight, white coat.

After I pay, I struggle through the door then consider walking off and pretending the strawberries are not mine. But waste is anathema to me, so I load them into the trunk and give most of them to the Salvation Army, along with a big check—hush money, I guess—before I drive home.

Delta's pacing—something she never does. Plus, she looks like she's been dunked with sixty-eight gallons of sweat.

"What the heck is going on?" I ask.

"Nothing."

"Listen, I've just made a fool of myself and you look like you've run to China and back. What are you trying to do? Kill yourself?"

She strips off a dripping T-shirt that says Obedience Takes All the Fun Out of Life, then marches down the hall.

Lord, I just realized the irony of Delta's T-shirts.

I pour two glasses of lemonade then sit at the kitchen table and see the headlines on the sports section of the newspaper: SEC Baseball Tournament in Hoover. Now I know why Delta couldn't stop running.

When she comes back wearing a generic white T-shirt, she says, "I've decided not to include Hoover's pork barbecue in my guide. We'll drive to Tupelo tomorrow. Check out Malone's fried catfish."

If there's one true thing I know, it's that Delta has to go.

"You're going to Hoover," I say. "We'll take the RV." Mike and I always drove the RV to games. It will be almost like old times.

"Can you drive it?"

"Yes."

Does once count? I'm not about to tell her the only time I drove the RV was out of the parking lot at Mississippi State where Mike and I had gone to see the Bulldogs play. Hoover's not that far. Surely I can manage a three-hour drive.

Finally, here is my chance to inch forward and Delta's chance to take a flying leap. Some call it courage, I call it faith.

CHAPTER 3

The heady scent of purple grapes ripening in the sun is as quintessentially Tuscan as baseball to a summer in America.

The Seasoned Traveler's Guide to Tuscany,
Delta Jordan

Delta

The first thing we hit backing the RV out of the driveway is Emily's hydrangea bush. When it flies past my window I take that as an omen.

"Let's not go, Em. That's a bad sign."

"The driveway's too short and it's just a hydrangea bush. I never liked it anyhow."

Next, I hear a crunch that's either the entire front of my Jeep Liberty Sport or the mailbox. Now the gods are screaming at me to turn around.

Or maybe it's my own fear.

It turns out to be the mailbox—once a lovely structure painted with a scene from Ducks Unlimited, now a crumpled mass attached to the side of the RV like a wart. It dangles precariously from one of the rearview mirrors then slides slowly downward and finds a new home under the chassis. Now we're going down the road accompanied by something that sounds like an Apache war dance.

"For Pete's sake, Emily. You can't even drive this thing."

"The hydrangea bush was not my fault, and I'd never have hit the mailbox if I hadn't been so upset about losing my blue robe."

Emily's spiteful cat sneaks over to claw my pants legs, while somewhere in the universe, white-bearded men in long flowing robes are taking notes and putting little black marks against my name.

"You didn't lose it, Em. I hung it in the basement closet. I was tired of seeing you in it."

"You hid it in retaliation. My Lord, Delta, nobody's going to *make* you go to a baseball game. I just don't want to see you giving up another single thing you need and want because of your father."

My mind tells me she's right while the rest of my insides are cringing like a scared child. And not because of her kamikaze driving.

"Road rage is so tacky," she says, as we careen past truckers who make rude gestures. "Look on the bright side, Delta. You might meet a cute baseball coach."

The only bright side I can see is that I'll be crushed to death in a motor home before her vicious cat eviscerates me.

If I ever do get where we're going I'm going to follow the advice she gave me when Larry left. "Just go off by yourself and scream. It releases all kinds of bad junk."

The thing is, once you release all your baggage, it's floating around in the open and you have to deal with it.

Emily

I always knew I could keep people entertained, but I never knew I was such a good actress till I made Delta think I was having a good time driving this RV through traffic in Birmingham Hades. Now I'm trying to park in the RV lot at Hoover Stadium where Mike and I spent so many great times with baseball-loving pals, and I'm telling Delta, "Relax. Just tell me if I get too close to the RV on my left." What I want to do is jump up and down tearing out big globs of hair and screaming for Mike.

He and I hardly ever missed a Mississippi State ball game, and being back in the thick of things makes me feel like I'm missing an arm or a leg. Besides, I'm forcing an issue here. Being within earshot of the stadium will make Delta have to face her baseball demons.

"Em, watch out!"

One more foot to the right and I'll be wearing the other RV. Good grief. It looks like the Whitworths' vehicle. I hope not. I don't want to mingle with our old sports buddies. I don't want commiseration and reminiscences and questions about my future.

I'm tired of being poor Emily at the center of every event. For the first time since Mike died I'm going to muddle through on my own.

Delta needs me, and it's my turn to drag her along in my tailwinds.

Delta

Emily's outside hooking up the RV and I'm sitting in a chair with my back to the window calling for a rental car.

"Are you okay?" Em prances by to wash her hands.

"I'm not going to jump off the Tallahatchie River Bridge so somebody will write a folk song about me, if that's what you mean. I'm going to take a quick run. The car's coming at five then we'll check out Full Moon Bar-B-Q."

I grab my running shoes and set out in the opposite direction from the stadium, but my daddy's voice is as clear to me as if he's running right alongside.

The game depends on his next swing.

It's just the two of us. It's the bottom of the ninth, the score is Mississippi State four, South Carolina six, State has two outs, the bases are loaded, and their best hitter is at bat with a full count.

I catch Daddy's excitement and squeeze my hot dog too hard, squirting mustard on the front of my T-shirt and down the inside of my arm. He wipes it off with the big white handkerchief he always keeps in his pocket, then pats me on the head and says, *We'll get ice cream on the way home.*

Sitting in the hot sun swinging my legs, I'm the most important person in the world. I'm going to grow up and become a baseball player because that's my daddy's favorite sport, and there's nobody I'd rather please than Carl Jordan with his big laugh and his dark eyes and his way of tossing you high in the air on summer nights when the fireflies are out and a million stars dot the sky.

I jerk myself away from this yawning crevice, put on some speed then run until I think I'll have to call Em to send somebody with a stretcher to get me.

When I get back, the car's already there, so after I change, Em and I head down Highway 31 to Full Moon Bar-B-Q. On the way she sings "Stars Fell on Alabama."

The restaurant lives up to its reputation, and we leave with our waistbands unbuttoned and the

T-shirts she insisted on buying. The Best Butts in Town, the slogan says.

"Your kind of shirt, Delta."

"I resemble that remark."

"I do, too, if you like backsides three ax handles wide."

As I drive through the humid Alabama night, this banter is a healing song, and I let its balm sink deep into my bones.

"I have two tickets for tomorrow's game," Em says. "You don't have to go with me, Delta, but I think you should. Until you confront your ghosts, you're going to keep getting baseball and relationships tangled up with Carl Jordan leaving you.

I start to say no, but the song is a balm that has sunk deep into my bones.

"Okay." I take a deep breath then say it again, because the word feels right, because I'm very tired of running.

When I wake up to the roar of fans from Hoover Stadium I almost change my mind. I almost tell Em I can't do this. But then I tell myself that after all these years I should be able to enjoy a sport I used to love. I should be able to sit through a game without feeling haunted by the ghost of a daddy I never really knew.

Em puts her hand on my arm. "Delta, I'm going to be sitting right next to you. Okay?"

"Okay."

I leave the safety of the camper and walk up the hill and into hot dogs and laughter, popcorn and excitement, school pennants and cheers, hard bleachers and heartache.

Emily grabs my hand, holds on tight, and I take a deep breath and wait for the toss of the first ball. Then the second and the third.

By the second half of the first inning, I relax, fall into the game, root for Mississippi State. But still, the memory of Daddy lingers.

"Are you ready to go home?" Em asks after the game is over.

"Yes."

"Okay. Me, too."

There should be a Hall of Fame for friends like her.

Emily

When we head home after the game I'm congratulating myself on two things: getting Delta to go to her first baseball game since her daddy left and becoming an expert at driving the RV. Now I'm whizzing past the sign that says Welcome to Mississippi and only one driver has made a fist at me the whole trip home.

Delta's kicked back in the passenger side, looking as relieved as somebody who just came through major surgery. "Tomorrow we'll drive up to Memphis to check out the ribs at the Rendezvous, and then we'll get our tickets for Italy."

I see right through her. She's trying to blackmail me, make me go to Italy because I made her go to Hoover.

"One ticket. I'm keeping my feet on terra firma. Besides, who would keep my cat?"

"Michele. Or Buddy Earl."

He always waters the flowers on my deck when I leave, and he'd keep Leo if I were going to Italy. Which I definitely am *not*.

Dark falls on us and shuts Delta up. She's the contemplative kind, always looking up at the night sky and trying to figure out what the stars and the moon are saying to her.

I've tried that, but so far the only time they spoke to me was when I blew a hole in my ceiling. I guess I shocked them into speech.

I beat her to the basement when we get home. I know what she's after, peace and quiet to organize her notes. But I'm after my blue robe.

The phone sends me scurrying back upstairs. It's Lucille.

"I'll bet you haven't even cleaned out his closet," she says before saying hello.

"I'm not ready to get rid of Mike's things yet."

"What? You'd let some poor old man freeze to death because you'd rather the moths eat Mike's wool sweaters?"

"His winter things are in mothproof closets, and I don't know any poor, freezing old men."

Delta comes up the stairs and I mouth "Lucille."

"You need some help," Lucille is saying. "I've got a bunch of boxes for Mike's clothes, and I'm fixing to buy some white paint. We'll clean out the closet first then spiffy up the house."

Paint my weathered cypress? Over my dead body.

"I'm fine, Lucille. Delta's still here."

"Pshaw! That girl's too skinny to swing a paintbrush. I've got plenty of hired hands who've promised they won't run the Double Bar J into the ground. I'm driving up Wednesday."

The bulldozer's running and I'm squarely in its path. There's not but one thing left to do: leap out of the way.

"I'm afraid it'll have to be some other time, Lucille. I'm leaving for Italy. My neighbor, Buddy Earl, will take charge of everything while I'm gone."

I feel like apologizing to Mike. He always wanted to take me to Venice to ride the gondolas and to London to see Big Ben. To Hawaii to see orchids growing wild. For Pete's sake, everybody goes to Hawaii.

Delta's still standing in the door watching me after I hang up.

"Don't look at me like that. I'm going. I said I would, and I am."

Later that evening lying in my bed with Leo's fat butt curved next to me, I see a single star shining through my window, the only star in a vast expanse of dark sky.

I wonder if it's Mike, trying to say hello.

Or is he trying to say goodbye?

CHAPTER 4

Pack light. One of the joys of international travel is leaving the familiar behind and learning to appreciate the unfamiliar.

The Seasoned Traveler's Guide to Umbria,
A work in progress, Delta Jordan

Emily

I've sunk so low in this seat nothing is visible from the back except a few tufts of my every-which-way hair. Flying on this paper airplane with the rubber-band rudders will be enough to turn me white overnight. Two weeks ago if I'd known I would be this terrified, I'd never have told Lucille I was going to Italy.

"Are you okay?" Delta asks.

I peep out of one eye and see her reading a thick book on the Etruscan period in Umbria as calmly as if she's sitting in her armchair instead of barreling through thick cumulus clouds so black you would think you're headed to Hades instead of Atlanta.

"If I get to Rome in one piece, I'm going to kill you."

"Okay."

"You needn't act so cheerful, Delta. I mean it."

"I know you do. But just wait till we're there. You'll be glad you finally decided to fly."

Actually, I already am. As opposed as I was to leaving Leo with Buddy Earl, as scared as I am that I'm going to plummet from the air like a wounded bird, I'm also grateful. If I hadn't told Lucille I was going, she'd have had her whole herd of cattle shipped up to Smithville and spent the rest of her days terrorizing both them and me with her hot branding iron.

Besides, I'm facing one of my fears head-on.

"Can I get you anything to drink?" the stewardess asks.

"Yes. Orange juice." I have to sit up a bit straighter to drink it. I even have to open my eyes.

But I draw the line at looking out the window. I did that once and nearly had a heart attack.

Now, thanks to Delta and Lucille, I'm a terrified international traveler. I'm praying with every breath that we don't crash on landing. The wheels connect with tarmac and we screech down the runway at the speed of light. Our pilot obviously just got out of training pants.

My exit from the plane is wobbly, but as soon as I get my land legs back I start feeling proud of myself.

Delta's striding through the airport wearing a backpack that I'm sure holds everything but a Porta Potty.

"Seasoned travelers pack light," she told me when we were packing.

Although she's the expert, I wasn't about to leave home without a pair of shoes to match every outfit. Mike never complained.

And so here I am plodding along like a packhorse with an oversized purse that weighs fifteen hundred pounds and an overstuffed carry-on that keeps tilting off its wheels. When I spot a rack that says Smart Carts, I grab one and load my possessions.

"Great," I say, then promptly run my smart cart up the robes of a Franciscan priest.

"Pardon me."

"No problem," he says. "Have a nice day."

I straighten up and hope I'm headed in the right direction. When I turn to ask Delta, I ram into the priest again.

"Sorry."

"It's okay."

Where is Delta? Well, if she can't find her way through an airport without my assistance, that's just too bad. I've got to catch a plane to Italy.

My smart cart gets out of hand again, and I bump into that same, long-suffering priest.

"Lady, if you'll pull that damned thing instead of pushing it, you might get where you're going."

Obviously you have to be smart to operate these things, and obviously I'm turning into the kind of woman who can make even a priest lose patience.

I look around expecting Delta to say something, but she's two gates back, laughing so hard she has to lean onto the wall for support.

I'm not waiting for her. I haul out of there as fast

as I can, *pulling* my cart, thank you very much. But Miss Long Legs catches me.

"Why didn't you tell me to pull it, Delta?"

"I was going to, but I didn't want to spoil the fun."

"Yours or mine?"

"I laughed so hard I think I've wet my pants."

"Serves you right."

Then I start laughing, too, and I realize this is the beauty and healing power of female friendships, the remarkable ability to laugh at ourselves no matter what the circumstances.

Delta

Umbria. The Green Heart of Italy.

We might have stayed in any number of quaint, charming cities but I chose Assisi because of the richness of its history and the spirituality that hangs in the air as clearly as the melody of cathedral bells. Our rented villa hugs the slopes of Mount Subasio just outside the Gates of Saint Francis. We overlook wide fields of brilliant yellow sunflowers on the plain below the city as well as the ancient olive grove adjoining the Sanctuary of Saint Damian.

Aren't sanctuaries where people go to heal? Maybe even to bloom?

While Emily sleeps off her jet lag, I discover the perfect room for writing, tall windows overlooking the courtyard, cool tile floors, lots of bookshelves and a huge, carved wooden desk. Throwing open the shutters, I lean out and listen to the birds and distant cathedral bells. Cypress trees swaying in the breeze seem to be dancing to the song of the bells.

If I ever put down roots, it could be in Italy. I feel connected here, a part of something large and wonderful and mysterious—a star, a tree, a breeze that whispers, *Rest now*.

"Delta?" Emily's standing in the doorway.

"Oh, good. You're up. Why don't you get dressed and we'll explore the city."

"You go ahead. Michele might call. Or Brennan. I need to stay here. I need to call Buddy Earl and check on the cat."

"I'm not leaving until you get out of that ridiculous blue bathrobe."

I'd have hidden it again if I'd known she was going to bring it to Italy.

She marches off, miffed, but I don't care. I guess I know a little about grief. After all, I lost my mother when I was forty-one.

And your father, a little voice says, but I ignore it.

There's a time to mope around and there's a time to pick yourself up and start living again.

Emily comes back in a peasant skirt and a pretty pink blouse. She looks like somebody who ought to be running wild through a sunflower field. Instead she sinks onto the love seat.

"You're not going to just sit there while I'm gone, are you? There's lots to do here, Em. The courtyard is fabulous, full of flowers and fresh herbs in pots. We have plenty of books, plus a wonderful stereo system. And the kitchen is magnificent. Almost fully stocked. I'm getting fresh fruit at the market. I know you love kitchens."

She jumps up, puts on an Elvis CD then starts singing along to "Don't Step on My Blue Suede Shoes." Until then I didn't know it was possible to sing and be disgruntled at the same time.

"There." She glares at me. "Is that better?"

"No. But at least you flew. And that's something."

I grab my sun hat and a good canvas bag for my notepad and the fresh produce I'll find at the open-air market then head out the door. If I knew the words to any songs, I'd sing them. That's how beautiful this place is.

But I'm not made that way. While Emily's wired for love and laughter and music, I'm made for career-planning and goal-setting and problem-solving.

As we were packing for Italy, Emily asked when I was going to retire, and I said, "Never."

The idea terrifies me. Retire to what? Travel? I do that anyway, and at the same time feel productive and needed. I know that sounds silly, but people depend on travel guides. They depend on me to tell them the best places to stay, the best restaurants, the not-to-be-missed sights. But mostly I think they depend on me for a sense of safety. My travel guides are maps, really, leading travelers through a maze of unfamiliar countries, assuring them that they are in charge, they know where they're going.

These guides make me feel useful, feel as if my life counts.

Larry said they were a crutch.

"You use travel writing as an excuse to run away," he told me in the last argument we had before he walked out the door for good.

"Run away from what, Larry? This is my career."

"You're never here to talk about us, about our future. I want to start a family."

"You know how I feel about that."

"I guess I figured that out when you didn't even take my name. And you flit off to Milan or Paris or Timbuktu every time I mention the word *baby*. Well, I've had it. I'm hitting the road, too. So long, see you in the book racks."

Why am I walking through these amazing olive groves thinking about ancient history? I have a job to do.

Assisi is a walking city. I've visited twice, briefly, and I'm thrilled for the chance to spend at least six weeks here. I love wandering the narrow curving streets and discovering its tucked-away shops and restaurants. Setting off down the hill, I head toward the Gate of Saint Francis that will take me through the walls and into the city.

My destination is the Temple of Minerva that

dominates the Piazza del Comune, a superb example of architecture of the Augustan period.

I walk the long flight of steps between Corinthian columns, enter the hushed splendor of the chapel and sit at the back, taking it all in. There's no need to take notes. I'll do those later. Right now I'm simply absorbing the ambiance, letting myself sink backward into an ancient time of religious fervor and colorful rituals.

Afterward I sit at a small table in the piazza sipping lemonade and jotting notes, my background music the sound of cascading water from the fountain, the flutter of pigeons' wings and the low hum of conversation as people swirl around me, unnoticed.

Over the years I've developed a technique for vanishing in a crowd. I can travel so far inside myself that, even if I look up, I don't see individual faces, don't hear snatches of conversation, don't even know where I am or what time it is, really. I'm in a place and a time all my own.

"A lady as lovely as you should be drinking Orvieto bianco, the prince of Umbrian wines."

Amazingly, I hear every word, look up and actually see the speaker, a man of such incredible good looks he can't possibly be real—tall and dark-eyed with a perfect face and body. He smiles, sets a glass of sparkling wine before me and another across the table, then slides into the chair as if I've been waiting here for him.

"Hello, I am Antonio Donacelli, and you are the most beautiful creature I've ever seen."

I have a full repertoire of retorts for men like him, strangers who think they can flatter me and get whatever they're looking for. I have a full range of withering looks that can send such men scuttling away with their tails tucked securely between their legs.

"I'm Delta Jordan."

All my sharp edges are softened by this sweet Italian sun and this handsome Italian Romeo. I smile at him, suddenly turning myself into a cliché, a needy American woman falling under the spell of a charming foreign man.

"And I am enchanted."

I believe he is. At least for the moment. And for the moment, I let myself float on the mellow mood that has overtaken me and the sharp, fruity taste of Orvieto bianco, the most famous wine in a region known for the simplicity and purity of its wines.

Today I'll enjoy this wine and by tomorrow this magical moment will have passed. They always do. I'll walk home to my rented bed in my rented villa and forget about the stranger who offered wine and flattery and stories about a town that fascinates me.

"What brings you here besides fate?" he says.

I know it's a line. I know I should get up and walk away. But I'm too jet-lagged and raw from dealing with memories of Daddy to consider leaving a half-finished glass of the best wine in Italy. So I tell him about my career, even name the places I've been and how each one was beautiful in its own way. "But none has ever come close to Italy."

If I didn't know better, I'd say I was trying to get to know him. A perfect stranger. *Perfect* being the operative word.

And would that be such a bad thing? A casual acquaintance who knows the real places in Umbria, telling me where to go next?

I've spent my whole life turning away from men like Antonio Donacelli. Men who were interesting and seemed to be kind. Men who might share a cup of coffee and talk about a great book and the world's best hiking trails and Puccini's greatest opera.

He's saying to me, "It's a pity you couldn't have been here for the Calendimaggio."

Spring Festival. He describes it in such vivid detail I can almost see the opulence and brilliant color, almost hear the music and taste the food.

Most people aren't that observant. I wonder what he does. But I won't ask, even out of curiosity because I don't want him to get the wrong idea. Italian men are renowned for taking a small show of interest and turning it into a romantic encounter.

"Next week I'll show you the historical pageant at Narni," he's saying. "We will dance in the street, then afterward hold hands in the moonlight."

All of a sudden I'm tired of petting dogs and picking daffodils and helping old men across the street. Alone. I'm tired of eating ice cream and being grateful.

I want somebody else to pick the daffodils and give them to me. I want somebody to help *me* across the street. I want to own the dog and the house with a big backyard that goes with it. I want to have somebody else buy the ice cream for a change, and I want to be grateful, but not just for that.

Em knows how to get all that, but I just sit in my chair as if somebody has rendered me stiff-backed and speechless with extra-strength glue.

"I don't know you."

"But you will, Delta Jordan. This I promise."

Men always break their promises to me. This much I know.

And so I don't tell him where I'm staying, won't let him walk me home, won't accept his offer of dinner or even more conversation.

"Thank you for the wine. I must be going."

His bow is formal, old-school charm. He even kisses my hand—another cliché—and when he straightens up I can tell by the look in his eyes that he felt me shiver.

Back at the villa Emily is standing barefoot on the cool tiles of our kitchen, chopping fresh basil on the marble countertop. A pot of pasta bubbles on the stove.

I congratulate myself. A kitchen has always been Emily's haven as well as her domain.

"Hi, I'm making basil pesto. Did you get fresh fruit at the market?"

"I didn't go to the market."

"Why not?"

I forgot? I didn't have time? Both lies tempt me, but in the end I say, "I met a man."

"Wow, he must have been a humdinger." She pours two steaming cups of cappuccino, sits at the primitive wooden table. I notice she's picked sunflowers, perfect for the brown pottery jar in the middle of the table.

This is amazing to me. She has always been a keen observer of nature, a woman who keeps every vase in her home filled—flowers in spring and summer, colored leaves in fall and stark, Oriental-looking branches in winter.

Since Mike died the lake house has been empty of those homey touches. It has been empty of music and the clacking of needles. Emily gives hand-crocheted afghans and hand-knit sweaters at Christmas. She can watch TV, carry on a conversation and knit a turtleneck pullover all at the same time.

Maybe I've finally rescued her, and now she can rescue me.

I tell her about my chance encounter, calling it *interesting* instead of *amazing*. Then I hold my breath waiting for her verdict.

"But he bought you wine, Delta. A perfect stranger in an Italian piazza. I think it's charming."

"Don't get carried away, Emily. I'm certainly not going to. Italian men are known for outrageous flattery and romantic gestures."

I change the subject, tell her about the great leather shop on the piazza, the one that sells Murano glass, the little bookstore that has remarkably beautiful notepaper as well as wooden marionettes of Pinocchio.

But long after she's asleep and the moon is high in the sky, much bigger and brighter than it has any right to be, I lean out the window and wonder what it would be like to walk underneath such a moon holding hands with a man. I wonder what it would be like to fall into the moment, to feel pretty and exciting and desirable, to let myself trust again.

CHAPTER 5

In the valleys outside the walled city of Assisi there are fields of sunflowers so large you can walk in them forever, surrounded by brilliant yellow blooms that make you think of being in the sun.

> *The Seasoned Traveler's Guide to Umbria,*
> A work in progress, Delta Jordan

Emily

Only my second day here and already I am on the phone with Lucille—who called in spite of international telephone rates and a tightwad nature—to warn me about *foreign devils.*

"I don't know why you let Delta drag you over there in the first place, Emily. Those foreign devils will take all your money and steal your virginity, too."

"What do you think I am? A babe in the woods and a self-rejuvenating virgin, to boot?"

"Oh, well, you know what I mean. When are you coming home? I can buzz up from Texas and be there in a blink. We still have lots to do."

"I'm afraid I'm losing the connection. Hello? Lucille? Lucille? I can't hear a thing. I'm hanging up now."

When I set the receiver back in its cradle, I don't feel the least bit guilty. I feel like a plant that has been in the greenhouse all winter and suddenly gets a sniff of spring.

I race upstairs for my raffia hat with the red ribbon trim, then stick my head into the sun-filled room where Delta's transcribing notes.

"I'm going to walk down the hill to those beautiful sunflower fields. Want to come?"

"No. I'm staying in today."

"Are you afraid of running into that handsome Italian?"

"I'm not afraid. I just don't want to waste my time, that's all."

"Delta, I've never regretted one single moment of joy that took me away from my work. And I'd give anything to have just one of them back."

I hurry out before she can think up a brilliant comeback, before I start spewing apologies. How did I ever get up the nerve to tell Delta how to live her life? Me? A woman who can't figure out how to live her own life.

I can't even decide what to do about my wedding ring, for Pete's sake. Last night after making basil pesto and starting to feel almost normal again, I took it off and put it in a velvet box in my purse. Then at three this morning I woke up in a panic and nearly broke my toe getting out of bed to retrieve it and put it back in its rightful place.

How can I expect to remove my wedding ring when I can't bear the thought of getting rid of Mike's clothes? And why should I?

Who does Lucille think she is, telling me what to do? Lord, she's run off every man that ever came within a ten-mile radius of her, including some of the best ranch foremen in Texas. Mike once said if Harold Franklin weren't hard of hearing and Lucille weren't blind as a bat without her bottle-bottom glasses, she'd have run him off, too. Fortunately, Harold never hears her call him a "dried-up buffalo turd not worth the poison it would take to kill a rat," and she never sees him imitate her bow-legged swagger and her flinty-eyed scowl.

Mike got all the looks in that family. If I didn't know better, I'd think his family had stolen him from gypsies.

Poor Lucille. I shouldn't be so uncharitable. On the spot I resolve to send her a gift. Or, better yet, I'll call home and have Michele send her some roses and a box of her favorite thin mints. After all, she's lost someone special, too, a brother she loved more than anybody else in this world.

By the time I've walked down the hill to the field of yellow flowers, the sun has cleansed me of remorse and replaced it with a feeling I can't define. Not contentment, but something close, a sort of peace that settles into my bones and seeps into my spirit and says, *There now, you can rest awhile.*

I walk deep into the field, and then stretch out with the flowers towering over me and the summer sun filtering through the leaves to make warm patterns on my skin.

"You would have loved this, Mike," I whisper.

I do, Emily. I do.

For the first time in days, I let myself cry. But these are not tears of pain for what I've lost; these are tears of joy for what I had.

I open wide my arms and my heart and give Mike back to the sun and moon and stars, to the perfect beauty and wonder of the universe.

Later that evening, I wake to the sound of music outside my window, lifting up through the star-studded night and filtering into my dreams of standing on my deck wrapped in Mike's arms while we watch a comet streaking across the dark sky.

Grabbing my robe, I run to the open window and lean over the casement. There in the moonlight is the most gorgeous man I've ever laid eyes on.

He has the melting romantic appeal of Antonio Banderas and the virile look of an Olympic athlete playing one of Italy's famous love songs on his guitar. Playing well, I might add.

The song is *"Amor ti vieta,"* and it tells the story of a man who has fallen in love with a woman whose eyes are saying yes while her lips are saying no.

I'm in love with this music, in love with the big Italian moon and the soft Italian night that promises life is not over. Love is not done with me. Wherever Mike is, wherever I am, we still have each other, forever engraved in our hearts and our memories.

I want to lean on this casement the rest of the evening, but out of the corner of my eye I see Delta arriving at her window, her hair a fiery halo in the moonlight. She looks like a heroine in a romance novel. She looks like a woman who knows the song is for her.

And it is. I would be selfish to stand here in plain view enjoying the music when I suspect—no, I know—the man in the courtyard below is none other than Antonio Donacelli and that he wants to play for Delta, alone.

I ease back into the shadows, listening to the tender love ballad and remembering how I met Mike, a sharp, savvy businessman while I was still a college kid on a summer holiday. I picture how he strode through Logan Airport with his briefcase, his wire-rimmed glasses and his stark white shirt while I grabbed Delta's hand and said, "Oh my gosh, he's coming our way." And when he saw me and smiled, I said, "I'm going to marry that man."

Just like that, I knew.

I wonder what Delta is feeling now. I wonder what she knows.

Some sixth sense sends me to her room just in time to see her leaving the window, reaching to close the shutters.

"Delta, don't."

"Why?"

"Go back to the window and just listen. We'll talk about it in the morning."

I can see the conflict in her face, imagine her thinking of the men who wooed and won her then walked away without a second glance.

"Don't think, Delta. Just follow your heart."

She moves back to the window while I tiptoe out of the room and down the stairs. This house has a huge library with deep, comfortable chairs and sofas, rich damask draperies and novels in English as well as Italian, French and German.

As I select a worn copy of *Wuthering Heights*, English version, I make up my mind that as long as I'm in Italy I might as well learn Italian. It's really a beautiful language. I'll start by paying attention when Delta speaks it instead of clowning around just putting an O on the end of every word.

The guitar music filters softly through the house, a perfect background for the novel I've read at least three times, a love story so heart-wrenching I lose myself in it every time.

"Emily?"

Delta's standing in the doorway in her white nightshirt featuring a sassy angel and a slogan that declares, Real Angels Don't Always Have Wings.

And suddenly I am struck by the bone-searing truth: good friends are like the mama eagles that fly underneath their eaglets till they learn how to trust their own wings. Some call them angels.

For weeks I've been gliding along in the draft of Delta's strong wings. Now *she* needs *me*. When it comes to relationships with men, she tucks her wings under and flounders around, forgetting she even has them.

It's high time to reverse roles. Although I'm not sure anybody will take a dumpy angel with unruly hair seriously.

"He's still out there. What am I going to do?"

She runs her hands through her hair, holds her head sideways as if it's too heavy to hold upright.

"Go outside and invite him in while I make cappuccino."

"I can't."

"Life doesn't come with guarantees, Delta. But I'll tell you one true thing—finding a good man, a man like Mike, is worth a million heartaches."

She's still standing there, caught in the kind of paralysis I'm all too familiar with lately.

"Go," I tell her, and miraculously, she races up the stairs and calls down to him from the window.

"Yes," I shout. "Yes!"

I don't even bother to change out of my blue

robe, not that I'd steal anybody's thunder, especially Delta's. Besides, he's not here to see me.

I measure coffee, reveling in the luxury of this kitchen that has every gadget known to man. The guitar music stops, then Delta comes back downstairs, this time in black leggings and a silky flowing purple top that makes her look like the queen of some exotic island.

"Quick, what do you think? Is this okay? Is it too casual, too over the top? Maybe I should change."

"Delta, slow down. Breathe. It's perfect, you look great and everything's going to be fine."

"You think?"

"Go. I hear him at the front door."

As she leaves I send a little prayer winging upward. Not a prayer, really, but a conversation with Mike. And maybe that's the same thing.

"Darling, I'm doing everything I can for her down here. See what you can do up there, okay?"

Suddenly there they are, a gorgeous man with beautiful eyes and a Delta I haven't seen in years, one whose face clearly says, *Okay, I'm not convinced but at least I'm willing to try.*

"I'm Emily."

"And I am honored."

Delta makes formal introductions, and he kisses my hand then moves back toward her as if she's the moon and he's the tide. A plus for him, in my book. When a man is with a woman, he ought to be totally with her. Every other woman in the room ought to fade into the wallpaper, be nothing more than a pale blur compared to the blazing comet in his hand.

I'm not an admirer of *Wuthering Heights* for nothing.

I hand him a cup of cappuccino then wait for Delta to pick up the conversational ball and run, but my articulate world traveler is suddenly acting like a charm-school dropout.

"So, tell me, Antonio," I ask. "What do you do?"

"I'm an artist, visiting my mother and aunts as well as showing some of my paintings at Galleria Le Logge."

I wait for Delta, the art lover, to jump in with a brilliant comment, but she merely smiles.

"Delta was reading some kind of art book on the plane coming over here. What was it, Delta?"

She finally rouses herself, and it's as if Rip Van

Winkle has come out of his twenty-year sleep and is making up for lost time. All of a sudden she's talking Michelangelo and Antonio's countering with Da Vinci, and I'm sitting at the table with a warm cup in my hands and a warm feeling in the pit of my stomach.

What if I hadn't come to Italy? I would have missed the sunflowers and the moonlight music and the chance to see this miracle unfold—Delta, blooming like a rose.

I know. *I know.* It's trite. But I'm no writer, and I'm most certainly no artist. I'm just an overprotected woman beginning to wake up after my own very long sleep.

CHAPTER 6

Umbria is a place of celebration.
The Seasoned Traveler's Guide to Umbria,
A work in progress, Delta Jordan

Delta

It's past midnight and I haven't once struggled to fill a lull in the conversation. He's fascinating, this olive-skinned man with the beautiful hands.

He also loves books. I haven't mentioned one yet that he didn't know. Part of me wants to race around like a little girl with a new kite in a March wind, but my cautious side screams, *It's a trick, an illusion. Unmask him.*

"I particularly love Eudora Welty's short story 'Why I Live at the P.O.,'" I tell Antonio.

Let's see how he does with a famous Mississippian.

"Using Sister's wonderfully comic voice was a stroke of genius. My favorite scene is the one where Stella-Rondo tells the family Sister wanted Pappa-Daddy to cut off his beard."

Astonishingly he launches into the scene, doing all the voices, quoting verbatim, if I'm not mistaken. Emily's in stitches and I'm amazed. Neither of my husbands would have been caught dead quoting a long passage from a book in public, or in private, either, for that matter.

He performs without embarrassment or hubris. And with a great deal of passion.

When he finishes his smile is easy and wide, and Emily claps.

"Bravo," I say, meaning it.

My husbands never read anything except the sports pages and the centerfolds of *Playboy* magazines. If you call that reading. After my second divorce, Emily said, "Delta, you didn't have a darned thing in common with them. They didn't even have library cards. Next time, check before you go off the deep end."

I guess I was so grateful somebody wanted to

stick around long enough to walk down the aisle I forgot about having a brain. And requiring one in my partner.

Not that I'm interviewing partners. But still, I can't help feeling a sense of satisfaction, as if I'm the one who has passed the test.

"I thought about being an actor," Antonio says.

"Why did you stop?"

"Lack of talent. Male pride. Two weeks into rehearsals I discovered all the men had female names for themselves and me. Behind my back they called me Roxanne."

"Oh, Lord," Emily says. "What did you do?"

I haven't seen her laugh this much since Mike died. Italy is pouring a healing balm on her soul. I steal a glance at Antonio, but he catches me redhanded. The long glance he gives me is frank and full of curiosity. And wonder.

Oh, help.

Sweat slides down my cheek and beads my upper lip. Some women get rosy-cheeked and dewy-eyed while I get sweaty thighs. No wonder I've never been crowned Queen of the May.

Finally Antonio turns toward Emily, but not before I'm wondering if I can discreetly hide my legs under the table and fan my skirts.

"Your friend is a delightful distraction," he tells Emily, and suddenly I'm wearing that crown. "But to answer your question, I told them I'd rather be called Sophia. That was the end of any more talk behind my back. And also the end of my acting career. I quit after the play closed."

Emily makes a move to stand, but I nod at her, no, and she reads my sign language. *Don't leave me alone with him*. Not that I'm afraid of Antonio. The one I'm afraid of is myself. There's too much here to start a woman dreaming. And there's far too much to break a woman's heart.

I don't domesticate well and neither do men like Antonio. Four walls and a mortgage can't confine them, and after a while routine stifles them. This I know. I married two exactly like him.

Well, not exactly. Antonio's familiarity with books has already blown that theory to bits. What I mean is, men who are so handsome three hundred women drop their pants the minute they walk into a room. Not discerning women, of course. Still, that's what it felt like to me while I was hitched to those two rolling stones.

"It's past midnight." Antonio kisses my hand. "Are you going to vanish once more and leave behind a glass slipper?"

"I don't recall leaving one on the Piazza del Comune."

"You left something even better. An indelible impression."

He sounds sincere, looks sincere. But he's an actor, after all.

Operating on sheer adrenaline, I escort him to the door.

"Good night, beautiful lady."

He doesn't say, *I'll see you again, I'll call*, but he asks for my cell phone number, brushes his hand softly down my cheek and I know he will, know I'll say yes. I battle the urge to close my eyes, lean into his palm. Instead, I remain upright and when he leaves I'm a kite twisting in the wind, first buoyed upward then tumbling toward the ground. He'll turn around, come back and say, *I made a big mistake. You're the wrong woman.*

But he doesn't. Still, I can't move. I'm under a spell, and if I make a sound, blink an eye, all this will vanish.

"Delta?" Emily puts her hand on my arm. "Are you okay?"

"I don't know. Things like this don't happen to me."

"It did happen to you, and you deserve it. Just keep telling yourself that."

After I go to bed the moon won't let me sleep. My room is filled with an impossible brightness. If I get up and close the shutters I also shut out the breeze and the dark outlines of tall cypress trees bending in the wind, graceful and resilient. There's a lesson to be learned from them. How to move with the elements and still remain rooted and strong, how to sway with the rhythms of the wind and make it look like dancing.

Emily

If I could get my hands on that Antonio What's-His-Name, I'd kill him. Delta and I both woke up this morning excited, and she's kept her cell phone in her pocket all day.

But he hasn't made a peep. What is he? Some kind of idiot?

"Don't worry, Delta. He'll call."

"I'm not worried. I'm going running before it gets too dark. Do you want to come?"

"No, I think I'll read. I want to finish *Wuthering Heights*."

She takes her cell phone with her when she leaves, and I go downstairs to curl up with Heathcliff.

When I wake up it's dark and I don't know whether it's morning or evening, and if I get up to try to find the light switch I'm liable to break my fool neck, so I just snuggle back down in this big, downy sofa and doze back off.

"Em?" I can barely see Delta's outline in the doorway. "Did you sleep down here last night?"

"Is it morning already?"

She says yes, and I tell myself that today I'll do better, but I don't think that's true.

Delta switches on the light, comes in and takes out her notes and starts working.

I notice her cell phone is nowhere in sight. When it comes to men, it takes so little to defeat her. *Don't give up,* I want to tell her, but after all, what do I know about Italian men? Maybe they're like Leo would have been if I hadn't had him neutered: yowling under every window. Maybe somebody ought to neuter this guy.

I call both my children. This is not as easy as it sounds. I never know whether Michelle is seeing patients in her office or at the hospital, and I certainly never know whether my dynamo son is in his office, in the courtroom, or at a high-powered political function with his wife Janice. She's a councilwoman in Pensacola. How they ever found time to have Joe and little Mike is a mystery to me.

Afterward, I go outside, fall into a chaise in the courtyard and watch two tortoises making their way toward each other. This could take awhile. Weeks, really, and I can just sit out here and vegetate, say I'm studying nature.

The truth is, I'm feeling guilty because I'm here and Mike's not, guilty I denied him the pleasure of foreign sights, guilty that I wasted thirty years.

* * *

The next morning I'm downstairs before Delta. I'm so proud of myself maybe I'll take up some exotic sport, bullfighting, for instance, though I've never admired the matador and always felt sorry for the bull.

I race into the courtyard and gather fresh basil for the scrambled eggs. A man older than God rides by on his bicycle, and I wave and yell good morning as if he's my long-lost uncle.

Delta leans out the window. "Do you want to go into Assisi with me? I thought we'd make a day of it, maybe have a picnic at the top of Mount Subasio."

"You want me to climb a mountain? I feel good, but not *that* good."

"It's only a small slope. We can walk it in forty-five minutes."

"Why would we want to walk a mountain?"

"You'll see."

Two hours later, armed with chunks of chewy bread, eggplant marinated in seasoned olive oil and the best Parmesan cheese in the world, I huff triumphantly to the top and am greeted by white doves. Dozens of them, fluttering around me like miniature angels.

"Oh," I say. Just that. *Oh.*

"Exactly. Look to your right, Em."

At first I don't see anything except the tall cypress tress that are everywhere in Assisi, but then I see it—a primitive wooden cross rising so high among the branches the tip catches the sun filtering through the leaves.

Nearby is a sprawled-out, ancient structure that looks like a church. Of course, every building here looks like a church to me.

"This convent is called L'Eremo delle Carceri or Hermitage of the Cells," Delta tells me, and I congratulate myself on being right. For a change.

"It was a favorite retreat of Saint Francis," she adds. "They say the doves are always here because of him."

All I know about Saint Francis is that he loved nature and I have a stone statue of him in one of my flower beds. Oh, and I know he's not Baptist because the first time Lucille saw him she said, "What are you doing with a heathen saint in your yard?"

If I had been Delta, I'd have said to Lucille, "Isn't that an oxymoron?"—which is what she later told me I should have said—but then, I'm not Delta.

Now she's saying, "I hope nobody takes out a cell phone while we're here," which is my sentiment exactly.

"If they do," I tell her, "I'll jerk it out of their hands, stomp on it and then box their ears. All very politely, of course."

"Woo, woo! You go, girlfriend." Delta pumps her arm in the air, then drapes it around my shoulders. "I'm so glad to see you getting your spirit back."

"I'm glad to see you letting yourself spend a lovely evening with a man."

"I'll never see him again."

The way she says this, bittersweet underscored with a sense of longing, I think Delta is asking me to contradict her, to make her believe that for once a good man has come into her life.

"Listen, Delta. I've been thinking about this.

Any man who goes to the trouble of finding out where a red-haired American woman in Assisi is

staying, and then rides up on a white stallion and sere-
nades her beneath her balcony is *not* going to vanish."

"I don't think he rode a white stallion."

I wiggle my eyebrows at her, a gesture that always
made Mike laugh, and she punches me on the arm
then asks if I want to go inside and see the hermitage.

"I think I'll wait out here."

Taking off my hat, I sit in the shade and listen to
the soft hum of doves, the flutter of wings, the wind
stirring the branches above me.

When we come down off the mountain, I feel as
if I'm still there, as if the tranquility of that place
has settled inside me and taken up permanent residence. We wander through shops piled high with
beautifully tooled leather, Murano glass and handmade hangings so beautiful they make you weep.
But it's the courtyards that catch my eye, the little
green spaces tucked into alleys and nestled against
the sides of ancient houses that call out to me.

An old woman with a red kerchief on her head
and a face as brown and wrinkled as a peach pit is
sitting inside one of them, a length of white yarn
pooled at her feet while she knits. I wave but she

just stares at me with eyes as dark and uninterested as a pool perch.

"I think I'll duck in here a minute," Delta says, and I'm about to follow when I see she's talking about the gallery Antonio mentioned where his paintings are on display.

As much as I'd love to see them, I want her to see them first, to have them all to herself, to stand in front of each one as long as she wants without feeling she has to hurry or turn around and say, Look at this.

"You go on, Delta." I sit on a stone bench outside the courtyard. "I think I'll sit here a minute and enjoy the sun."

Delta

I'm almost afraid to go inside, afraid I'll run into Antonio and he'll think I'm trying to find him. Or worse yet, that his work will be dark canvases slashed with angry reds and muddy browns, filled with severed legs and floating eyeballs, reeking with rage and despair.

I don't let myself look at the names on the

plaques; I just follow my eye, my heart. A huge canvas on the back wall draws me, a scene of such compelling beauty I want to dip my toes in the painted stream and turn my face to the sun I know is just out of sight, just beyond the overhanging branches of cool, green trees. Light pours through this picture. And something else, too. Hope.

"The artist is Antonio Donacelli." A tall, elegant woman with gray streaked through her careful bun is standing at my elbow, speaking in perfect English. "He's internationally renowned and his shows sell out very quickly, so if you want that one, I'd advise you to get it today."

I glance at the brass plaque, confirm that Antonio painted this magnificent, life-affirming piece.

"I'm just looking," I tell her.

"When you consider his masterful use of light and shadow and the way he borrows from the French Impressionists and yet maintains a strong style of his own, the price is very reasonable."

"It's not the price. I don't have a house."

"I'm sorry," she says, then walks away.

Suddenly I no longer see myself as unencumbered and free, but rather as a woman who has gone through life missing out on the best things—walls on which to hang exquisite works of art, a kitchen filled with the smell of yeasty bread, and someone to hold my hand and say, You don't need these socks, then let me tuck my cold feet against his warm legs.

CHAPTER 7

Umbria is a region of great art. Knowing the names of artists such as Andrea della Robia is a plus, but the best way to appreciate a magnificent painting is to share it with a friend or lover.

The Seasoned Traveler's Guide to Umbria,
A work in progress, Delta Jordan

Delta

I leave the gallery almost blinded by the beauty of Antonio's art and the power of my own insights. When I don't see Emily, I immediately think she's wandered off.

Then I hear her. "Delta. Yoo-hoo! Over here."

She's sitting in a private courtyard beside an ancient woman, and the two of them are knitting.

If I didn't know Em so well I'd wonder how she managed to communicate without speaking a word of the language, but it doesn't take a genius to see that all she needs is her smile and a few gestures.

"Tell Rosa I said thank you, Delta, and that I want to come back tomorrow, if she doesn't mind. Oh, and ask her the name of the shop so I can get some knitting needles and yarn."

Rosa is happy to have the *"bella Emilia"* return.

"Bella means beautiful," I tell Em.

"I know that. I saw *Lady and the Tramp*."

She starts singing *"Bella Notte"* right there in the middle of the street, and people stop to smile and wave as we wind around the piazza and down a narrow alley to purchase knitting supplies.

Afterward we make our way through the gate where the sunflower fields spread out like a golden carpet. As if we've read each other's thoughts, we head that way, arm in arm. Wading through flowers taller than our heads we suddenly start whirling and spinning like butterflies.

We used to do this as children, spread our arms wide and twirl for the sheer joy of movement, of living. I wonder when we stopped, and why. I wonder if being in this place where nobody knows us, nobody watches, nobody judges, has sprung a latch and set those children free.

Whatever the reason, I'm glad. Constantly being grown up is a wearisome task. If I take nothing else home it will be this: Don't be afraid to let go and dance in the sunflowers.

When we finally make our way up the slope to our villa, two letters are waiting, the one on top with a return address from Huntsville.

· "You have letters from your children, Em." I hand them to her. "I'm going into the office to work a while."

I hang my sun hat on the hall tree and kick off my shoes so I can feel the cool tiles. In my office the late-afternoon sun slants through a bank of west-facing beveled-glass windows and makes miniature rainbows on the walls.

"Em, come quick. You have to see this."

When she comes in I'm dancing once more, barefoot and hedonistic, the lesson of the sunflowers taking hold.

Emily kicks off her shoes and joins me.

Finally we collapse on the sofa, giggling and winded.

"I almost forgot." She hands me one of the letters. "This is yours. From Antonio."

In this day of quick communication and instant gratification, writing letters is a dying art. I study the envelope as if I've unearthed an artifact. Antonio's handwriting is big and bold with tiny gaps in the middle of words, which means he lifts his pen and creates each letter as carefully as if he were painting a masterpiece. The paper is cream-colored and heavy, rich in texture. Handmade, I'm guessing. Did he make the paper himself or did he go to a specialty shop and stand in front of the displays selecting the exact paper he thought would please me?

"It's beautiful."

"Open it, Delta. I'm dying of curiosity."

"It might be private."

"Oh, for Pete's sake. If you're too chicken to open it, let me."

How did she know? How could she guess I was thinking he must be writing a Dear John letter? I

know it sounds silly, ditching somebody before
you've even started anything. Still, he's an artist. He
would write to be sure I get the picture.

Now I'm making nervous puns. What next? A
Seasoned Traveler's Guide to Getting Dumped?

"Let me find a letter opener."

I'm not about to tear into this beautiful paper,
mar the return address, leave ragged edges.

"Well, what does it say?"

I start reading in Italian and Emily flounces from
the room. Actually, Antonio wrote the letter in
perfect English.

Dear Delta,

My first impulse is to stand underneath your
bedroom window and serenade you every evening until you either fall passionately in love
with me or throw the dirty dishwater on my
head. My saner side—I do have one, you
know, in spite of the fact that I am Italian—
is to let you settle into your villa and your
work, then make myself indispensable to you.

I know you want to cover every aspect of

Umbrian culture in your guides, and who better to show you the great works of art than I?

I will arrive at your door at eleven o' clock in the morning and we will view the Italian masterpieces together. Holding hands. This I promise.

Yours,

Antonio

"Well, what did he say?" Emily's standing in the doorway, not the least bit sheepish. When I tell her, she says, "You're going, of course."

"How can I refuse? An artist as a tour guide for art?"

"If he had invited me, you can bet your sweet patooty I wouldn't be thinking of him as a tour guide."

How easy for Emily, who has known nothing but love and acceptance. If I start thinking beyond Antonio as a tour guide I'll get tangled in my past, and that's a place I'd rather not visit.

"The two most important paintings in this room are *Madonna and Child* by Duccio di Buoninsegna and *Crucifixion* by Maestro de S. Francesco," Antonio is saying.

We are in the National Gallery of Umbria, which is on the third floor of the Prior's Palace, and I'm surrounded by magnificent paintings of the Umbrian school dating from the thirteenth to the nineteenth century. But the thing I notice most is the warmth of his hand holding mine.

It was so natural, this joining of hands. Like two doves nesting together in the eaves of the convent at the peak of Mount Subasio. He met me at the door of my villa this morning and we drove to Perugia, just two people testing each other for friendship. Then he opened my car door and took my hand and hasn't let go since.

I don't want him to. I don't think about why. I just let myself fall into the moment and float.

We tour every gallery, every cathedral, every Etruscan arch of Perugia, stopping only long enough to eat pasta with basil pesto at an outdoor café facing the famous Fontana Maggiore, the Great Fountain, with its twenty-four red marble bas reliefs.

Then late in the evening he drives to a high green hill to show me a panoramic view of the sprawling medieval city at sunset.

"Thank you," I say.

He kisses both cheeks and says, "The pleasure was mine, beautiful lady."

He doesn't come in for coffee, doesn't say he'll see me later, and I go inside the villa torn between gratitude for the tour and disappointment for... What?

Someone to hold my hand, I'm thinking. Just that. The simplicity and comfort of touch.

"Where's Antonio?" Emily's barefoot, dressed in a yellow sundress and trailing a knitted length of red yarn that stretches from here to Texas.

"His mother and aunts were waiting for him. Did you roll out the red carpet for me?"

"It's a scarf, smarty pants," Emily answers. "Just for that I shouldn't tell you, you have a letter."

It's from Antonio, and I am fascinated. What manner of man is this? Certainly not like anyone I've ever known.

Dear Delta,
Tomorrow we will drive to Lago Trasimeno where I will have a sailboat waiting. The lake is surrounded by olive groves and is very peaceful. I'll take you to the north shore and tell you the

history of the famous battle where Hannibal's
Carthaginian army defeated the Romans.

A day of play is exactly what the doctor or-
dered, as you Americans are fond of saying.
Afterward, we will retrieve Emily and drive to
Spoleto where we will see *Forever Tango*.

Yours,

Antonio

I read his letter aloud to Emily, and she says, "Of
course, you're going."

"You make it sound so easy."

"It is, Delta. Just listen to your angel."

"Who would that be?"

"Me."

Over bruschetta, Emily tells me about her day
with Rosa, knitting.

"Maybe I'll open a little shop when I get home.
Someplace where women who love to sew and
crochet and knit can come and find exquisite yarns
and lengths of lace and exchange patterns and
stories. Every hand-worked piece has a story. I wish
I knew Rosa's."

"I'll go with you and find out."

"Not tomorrow."

"No. Not tomorrow."

After Emily and I say good-night, I sit in the middle of my bed and read Antonio's two letters again. He never bothers to ask if I'm available or if I want to go. He just tells me. If he were any other man I would call this arrogance and hubris.

But he's not any other man. He's a talented, disarming man with warm hands that held on to mine and made me feel like a woman set free.

From what, I don't know. And I don't want to think about it. I just want to lie in this bed and let everything I feel show. I wonder if it does. I wonder if Emily saw it in my face.

CHAPTER 8

If you travel to Umbria to see the historical
and artistic wonders but miss the mystical,
you've missed the best part of your journey.
  The Seasoned Traveler's Guide to Umbria,
        A work in progress, Delta Jordan

Delta

We are in a polished wooden sailboat, ancient I
think because they use fiberglass now, white sails
billowing in the wind, the only boat on the lake.
Olive groves surround us on three sides, and the vast
plain on the fourth faces toward Tuscany.

Antonio tells me about his wife, an aspiring opera
singer who died at the age of twenty-four. He talks
about his large family—four brothers, two sisters, his

mother, Gina, and seven aunts and uncles. He makes them sound like people I'd enjoy knowing.

I feel a bit self-conscious that I can only reciprocate with stories about the men who left me, and so I stick to my career. I tell him about my time in Tuscany.

"I fell in love with Florence when I saw Puccini's opera *La Boheme*. There's something so hauntingly beautiful about his music, I cry every time I hear it."

"Good," he says, then lowers the sails so we are drifting, takes his guitar out of the case and starts playing.

It's probably the only song I would recognize out of his repertoire—and only because it's from *La Boheme*.

I lean against cushions as blue as the lake while Antonio starts singing. "*Che gelida manina.*" Good Lord. How is it possible for a woman my age to feel as if this Italian love song was written especially for me? My bones have vanished. I feel light-headed. He's going to think I'm crazy.

I close my eyes so he won't see what I'm feeling, what I'm thinking. They say eyes are windows of the soul, and if this is true I'm far too old to parade my soul around in front of this too-sexy, too-handsome, too-talented, too-romantic man. Oh, and did I mention too young?

Not that I know his age, and he most certainly doesn't know mine. Emily says you can't trust a woman who tells her age: if they'll tell their secrets, they'll tell yours.

"Beautiful lady," Antonio whispers.

His hands are on my face. Lord, when did the music stop? And how did he get to my side of the boat without dumping us both into the water? And what am I going to do about his lips, which are on mine? Hot and talented. Did I say that?

Oh, and did I mention that I'm kissing him back? Not sedately, either. Suddenly I'm Madame Bovary and Blanche DuBois and every other famous fictional lover you've ever read about.

And I don't care. Did I say that? I've completely lost my mind as this magnificent man does things that make me feel as if I've been reborn.

Emily

If there's anything in this world sexier than the tango, I don't know what it is. Well, yes, I do. It's watching the tango performed in the ruins of a Roman theater with a full moon as a backdrop. Not a prop. The real thing.

And, oh yes, watching your best friend's face as she sits beside you with an Italian heartthrob holding her hand. She didn't have many lines on it to begin with, unlike me, whose face looks like chickens scratched a road there, but those she does have are now softened and practically invisible.

I wonder what happened on that Lake Whatyoumacallit.

As soon as we get home I don't beat around the bush. We fix ourselves two cappuccinos, get comfortable in the kitchen and I ask her.

"We sailed all day, stopping to see some of the sights. Antonio knows history as well as he does art. I'm getting tons of information for my guide book that would have taken me days to discover by myself."

"Shoot, is that all?"

"No, that's not all."

My Lord, she's actually blushing. But I'm not fixing to make a federal case out of this. Best friends ought to tell each other everything except that.

Intimate details. Those are best kept secret and savored in private.

Even though I'm dying of curiosity, I'm not fixing to deprive Delta of that. After all these years. *Hallelujah!*

"I suppose that means you'll be going somewhere again tomorrow?" is what I say.

"No. tomorrow I'll go with you to find out Rosa's story. Tomorrow night we'll go to Antonio's opening at the gallery. 'Night, Em."

She heads up the stairs. It's all romantic and wonderful and I feel like I'm sixteen, watching my best friend discover love. I hope. And isn't it amazing that such a thing could happen at our age?

Rosa's courtyard is filled with enormous Italian urns—what else?—and little primitive benches made of a thick slab of wood atop sturdy stones. Hydrangeas are blooming everywhere and water cascades from an ornate fountain that I'd give my eyeteeth for.

I wonder if I can find one and Delta can help me have it shipped back home. I've decided I'm too lazy

to learn Italian, after all. As long as Delta's around
to do my talking, why should I bother my brain?

I'm learning new knitting stitches. That ought
to be enough.

I'm doing a rather difficult popcorn stitch now
while Delta interprets the musical rise and fall of
Rosa's speech.

"She's eighty-seven years old and her husband
was killed in the Second World War."

"Tell her I'm so sorry."

Delta translates and Rosa nods, then continues
with her story.

"She had three children and they're all living in
other parts of Italy and are too busy to worry about
an old mother with arthritis and a sinking
shoulder."

"Tell her she has my sympathy. What's a sinking shoulder?"

"I don't know. Do you want me to ask her?"

I tell Delta no, and she continues following
Rosa's sad saga. That's what I'm calling it now,
because compared to my life, she's earned her right
to sit in the sun the hard way.

"She says you are like a daughter to her and she wants you to come back at Christmas and on her birthday, even if you don't bring gifts, which she likes but does not require. She just wants you to know."

"When's her birthday? Tell her I'll come, bringing gifts."

Rosa claps her hands as Delta relays this news, and all of a sudden I'm a woman planning to rack up frequent flyer miles. Maybe I'll learn Italian after all. Or I might just get a book that tells me the words for *Please* and *Thank you* and *Where's the toilet?*

Tomorrow I'm going to take Rosa a bag full of sunshine-yellow yarn. I don't have to know her language to tell her it's a gift.

When I get home, I race down the hill and dance among the sunflowers while Delta's holed up with her computer. Except for Rosa's courtyard, this is my favorite place. Mike's always here, whispering to me on the wind that nods the giant yellow blossoms. Not words, really. Just lovely affirmations. Sweet assurances that he's always with me. And he's applauding.

I walk slowly back up the hill, stopping in the

olive grove on the side of the hills long enough to marvel at how these small, twisted trees could survive centuries of man's foolishness. That's how old Antonio said they are. Centuries.

I say to them, "If you can do that, I ought to handle another thirty years or so."

But I don't want to merely survive. I want to triumph. To live with grace.

And what is grace, really, but acceptance and gratitude, understanding we are part of this vast, wonderful universe, and being thankful.

When I return, Delta's gorgeous in a flowing green dress that brings out her eyes and makes her look about ten feet tall. I grab my good jewelry and something that makes me look like a flour sack. Nobody's going to notice me at the art gallery anyhow. If it weren't for Delta I'd be holed up in the library with another hero comparable to Heathcliff. Rhett Butler, maybe.

At the gallery, Antonio kisses my hand, then starts to whisk Delta away.

"Em, will you be okay?"

"Go. If I were any more okay I'd be turning cartwheels."

I weave my way through the crowd, heading toward the nearest corner.

"Emily? Emily Jordan?"

The voice coming from my left is definitely American. I turn toward a tall man I don't know. Curly gray hair. Fragrant pipe.

"It *is* you."

He takes both my hands and I recognize the square jaw, the blue eyes.

"Clifford Booth."

My old flame. Pre-Mike. Pre-college. Pre-everything, really. Clifford was my first high school crush. I was fifteen, he was eighteen. Captain of the baseball team. I used to sit in study hall and practice writing "Mrs. Clifford Booth, Emily Jordan Booth, Mrs. Cliff Booth."

It was two thousand years ago. It was only yesterday.

I stand up straighter, suck in my stomach. Smile.

I think that this kind of female preening is called hope.

Delta

My body is here amidst the glitter and glamour of the gallery, but my real self is somewhere above me shaking its head.

Careful, it's saying, while Antonio is saying, "This is my sister, Sophia."

She's like him, too gorgeous to be true. Charming. Socially adept. I feel as awkward as a Muscovy duck.

Grabbing another glass of wine from the tray of a passing waiter, I leave the burden of conversation to them. Maybe I'll write another book, *The Unseasoned Traveler's Guide to Being a Wallflower*. I'm acutely aware of every year I've spent with my computer while the Emilys of the world are out dancing.

"Delta, there's somebody else I want you to meet, a good friend of mine, an art aficionado." Elegant, I'm picturing, fat pocketbook and slim hands, polished patent evening shoes. "I met him in New York ten years ago when I had my first showing there, and we've visited each other every summer since then. He's an American."

Paunchy, I revise. A fondness for cheeseburgers with French fries. Sturdy brown shoes.

He leads me across the room and introduces Clifford Booth, who is posturing beside Emily as if he owns her.

Good Lord. Cliff was an arrogant show-off, always posturing around in his baseball uniform. What if he's an opportunist, as well? Emily's wearing two carats of diamonds in her ears and another three on her fingers.

"Long time no see, girl."

Girl? I glance at Emily to see how she's enduring this jackass, but she's smiling and serene. I've always thought of her ability to pretend as a handicap, but now I envy it. It comes in handy in social situations like this when you're with a man you thought you knew, a man you've had *sex* with, for goodness' sake, and all of a sudden you realize you don't know him at all. He has this whole other life that includes people you've never liked.

While the three of them chat I feel as if I'm drifting off on a strong current. I try to anchor myself by looking over Emily's shoulder at my favorite of all Antonio's paintings. *Speranza*. Hope.

The thing we cling to until our fingernails are bloody and we can't hold on anymore.

And what is hope, really, except the fiercest love we hold?

I grab on with both hands, try to hang on, but when the crowd thins and Antonio steers me into an empty alcove it slips from my nerveless hands, falls to the floor with a crash that only I can hear.

"Delta, I've taken a room for the evening at the Il Palazzo," Antonio whispers.

Medieval charm, balconies overlooking the Spoletana valley, an antique bed for an uncertain woman and a man she knows nothing about. Not really. What is his favorite song? His favorite movie? His favorite toothpaste? Does he sleep in pajamas so nobody will see him naked when he goes to the kitchen in the middle of the night for a peanut butter cracker? Does he even like peanut butter?

"I have to go back to the villa with Emily," I say.

Antonio cups my face, seduces me with his dark eyes, leans his forehead against mine so his wine-sweet breath stirs my hair. If he kisses me I'll be lost. I won't have a brain cell left to say, *I made a mistake, let's just shake hands and be friends*.

"Some other time, then," he says. And as he turns to leave, "I promise."

I don't shake hands after all. I lean against the wall until I can walk without falling, then I find Emily and hightail it back to the villa.

Lightning is stabbing the sky and the distant roar of thunder promises a deluge. I've always thought thunderstorms would be perfect for cuddling under the covers with somebody to love. If I had somebody to love. Who loved me right back. That's the key.

"I'm going to have dinner with Cliff tomorrow."

"What do you know about him, really, Em? After all these years?"

"I've sort of kept up. His sister and I exchange Christmas cards. He coached for a while, then left to take a John Deere dealership. He's been very successful."

"I didn't know any of this."

"You were busy. Listen, Delta, I'm not the dumb blonde everybody likes to think I am."

"I never thought you were dumb, Emily, and you were never a blonde. You were brunette."

"Bleach counts. I may dye my hair honey-blond when we get home."

"Good Lord, because you saw Clifford Booth?"

"No, just because."

Suddenly we both sag onto the sofa, our feelings too heavy.

Oh, who do I think I am, trying to advise Emily when I can't even figure out how to get up the stairs and take my clothes off, much less what to do about a false-start love affair.

"It's not a date." Em twists her wedding ring. "It's too soon after…"

Her voice is as shaky as I feel. I reach for her hand and we sit side by side, not saying anything for a while. The wind picks up, slaps shutters against the side of the house and whistles around the eaves.

"I don't think I can go with Cliff. What would people say?"

"Em, we're in *Italy*. And who gives a rat's behind what anybody back home would say anyhow?"

"Except my children. I don't want them to think

I'm being disloyal to their father. I don't want to be disloyal to Mike."

"Your children love you. They'll be supportive, whatever you do."

"Then there's Lucille. She'd be on me like a Texas tornado."

"Forget Lucille. This is your life, Em, not hers."

"Thank God."

Never go to bed crying. That has always been Em's and my motto. We head up the stairs, and I pull the covers close under my chin while the rain lashes the roof and winds moan around the windowsills. It sounds like somebody crying.

It sounds like me.

CHAPTER 9

When I was researching this guide I let myself get sidetracked by the sound of blues coming from Beale Street. If I hadn't, I would have missed some of the best music this side of heaven. Go on. Take a chance. Get sidetracked.

The Seasoned Traveler's Guide to Memphis,
Delta Jordan

Delta

Emily went into town this morning to buy yarn for Rosa, and then she was going to sit in the courtyard with her friend and knit.

I offered to go with her to the shop but I'm glad she said no. Merchants here are accustomed to people who don't speak the language. She'll manage just fine.

Anyhow, I don't want to go anywhere near the Piazza del Comune, near the art gallery. I just want to work, to forget.

The rains polished everything, and outside my window the cypress trees are so green and fresh, they look reborn. They tug me away from my desk and I see the postman delivering mail.

For me, as it turns out.

Dear Delta,

You are an orchid, exotic, exquisite and fragile-looking. But I know that orchids have tenacious roots and need only air and moisture and the bark of a good tree to thrive.

I want you to bloom in a different place, in the rich pleasures I can give you, in banquets of succulent *fettucine al profumo di bosco* and in all the splendors of my county.

I have rented a hot-air balloon. We will mount the skies this evening before dusk, and I will watch wonder on your beautiful face.

Yours,

Antonio

I fold the letter and place it back in the envelope. My mouth is watering. And not merely for smoked, wood-flavored pasta with truffles. I want everything Antonio offered. And more.

I want to be the kind of woman who believes she is meant to have every good thing and who is not afraid to reach out and take it.

"Delta? What's wrong?"

Emily's back with a bag of golden yarn under her arm, but she's asking the wrong question.

"Antonio's coming."

I say it just that way. *He's coming.* Not, *He wants me to go,* but *I don't know if I will.*

I want to be Antonio's orchid and fly to heaven in a hot-air balloon.

"I knew he would." She grabs my hands. "Oh, Delta. You *deserve* this."

While we have a late lunch, I chant her words to myself like a mantra. I say them until I almost believe they're true.

As we hurl toward the heavens in a hot-air balloon the colors of the rainbow, Antonio watches me in the way I've seen other men look at other women. I wish I could see myself as he sees me. I wish I could look beyond the scared little girl, the socially backward woman and see a woman worthy of such adoration.

We're high above cathedral spires and cypress trees. Mountains washed pink by the sunset are at our backs while Assisi and the plains of sunflower fields spread out below.

Antonio holds my hand while I lean over the edge of the basket, awed. I wish I could live in this balloon. I wish I could spread my arms and hold onto this peace and harmony and grandeur forever.

"Thank you," I say.

"It's my gift to you. And it comes without obligation."

I don't say thank you again. Here in the romance of the sunset skies, I want to lie down in the middle of the basket and spread my skirts like the petals of a fallen flower.

But the basket is rapidly descending now, the sides of the balloon collapsing as we make our way back to the earth. Once we're on the ground, I know how to plant my feet. I know where my shoes are and I know exactly which way to run.

Emily

Cliff and I are in a restaurant whose name I can't pronounce, looking at a menu I can't read. Maybe this is why I never wanted to fly. No matter where Mike and I drove in the continental U.S., I could always read the menu.

"This is the best restaurant in Assisi," Cliff says.

Well, any fool who has ever set foot out of Smithville, Mississippi, could tell that. It has vaulted brick ceilings and real linen napkins and heavy cutlery and waitstaff just standing around hoping you'll crook your little finger.

Mike would have loved it. Guilt pricks me. I bury my face in the menu, pretending to be absorbed. My husband looms large, a benevolent shadow I can almost reach out and touch, a hovering spirit with hands that sometimes brush against my cheek right before I fall asleep. This love is so palpable I feel it inside me like a second beating heart.

"Mike used to love discovering new restaurants," I tell Cliff.

There. That ought to put this evening in perspective. That ought to tell him this is no date, this is not cheerleader Emily picking up where she left off with star athlete Cliff Booth.

He sits forward, interested, not at all surprised or uncomfortable that I want to talk about my husband.

"Tell me about your husband, Emily."

I tell him everything I know that was wonderful and good about Mike while Cliff sits back in his chair, a model of understanding and genteel Southern manners. I'm not aware of the tears, but he leans across the table to hand me his handkerchief so I wipe my face without interrupting the flow of words, the story of a marriage so miraculous I'm still shocked that death could end it.

"I was one of the lucky ones," I say. "I've seen couples in restaurants who don't even speak to each other except to say 'pass the salt.'"

"You are. I left both my wives so we wouldn't end up hating each other."

I'll edit this part out when I tell Delta about my date.

Oh, Lord. I'm sorry, Mike.

Of course, Cliff's not a date. Just an old friend taking me to dinner in a foreign country.

I hide my discomfort behind the menu, then feel Cliff's hand on mine, lowering it so he can see my face.

"Emily, this evening is not about a second chance with the one true love of my life. I loved both my wives. Wouldn't have married them if I hadn't. But when you reach a certain age, it's hard to find a woman whose company you enjoy, let alone a woman who's not after your money."

"I'm not after yours, Cliff."

"That makes us even. I'm sure as heck not after yours."

What tipped him off? My diamonds? Or maybe his sister? Compared to the rest of the world's metropolises, the cities in northeast Mississippi are so small everybody knows everybody else's business. And most of them don't mind telling it.

"If you can read this darned menu, order for me, Cliff. All of a sudden, I'm starving to death."

"I like my women with a healthy appetite."

"I'm not your woman, and if you want to hang out with me you'd better quit acting like the star of a high school baseball team and start acting like a grown man."

Cliff has this great big laugh I remember and enjoy. And I'm not going to feel guilty about that. Laughter is a good thing.

"It's hard to teach a stubborn old bulldog new tricks, Emily. But I want to hang out with you, and I'll do my best to behave."

"If an old bulldog can stand a filly who's never been anywhere but the barn, I'm game. Where do we start?"

"Why don't we start with *bruschetta al tartufo nero di Assisi?*"

"The only thing I know about all that is the bread, but I think that's as good a place as any to start."

Delta

The bed at the Il Palazzo is antique, just as I thought it would be. There's a great view of the Spoletana valley in the moonlight. But it's not the valley that absorbs me. It's the strong shoulders and dark eyes of the man above me.

I am still floating in the balloon.

Emily

When I say good-night to Cliff I feel my silk skirt against my thighs and my hair curling against the nape of my neck. I smell my own perfume—the gardenia fragrance Mike loved—and I feel my own femininity, the woman inside my skin who is clamoring, *I'm still alive*.

Inside the villa, Delta's in her nightshirt that features a box of bonbons and the slogan Eat More Chocolate. I take that as a good sign. She's usually in a good mood when she wears it because she has followed the advice of her own nightshirt.

Sure enough, she pats the seat beside her and offers me the other half of a chocolate bar.

"Tell me everything," she says, and I do. Except the part about Cliff leaving two wives.

"Did he try to make a pass at you?"

"What kind of question is that?"

"The Cliff I remember was a hellion, a bad boy always looking for trouble."

"For Pete's sake, Delta. He was an athlete. A star pitcher."

"Well, don't you be his next score."

"I'm going to bed."

"Emily…"

"I'm not talking to you."

The bad thing is, I really do want to talk to Delta. Maybe she can help me understand these conflicted feelings. How can I love Mike with every fiber in my being and with Cliff Booth, feel like a woman coming awake after a long sleep?

I put on my gown then go to the window and lean out to see if I can find the stars, to see if I can find answers.

To see if I can find Mike.

But all I see is a sky full of clouds that obscure everything except a small corner of the moon.

I'm looking everywhere for direction except inside myself. Whatever happened to that woman who danced in the sunflowers? And what happened with Delta tonight? I was so engrossed in my own story—as usual—I forgot to ask.

Grabbing my robe, I scoot down the hall to her bedroom.

"Is that you, Em?"

"Yes."

"Come on in. Turn on the light." She pats a place beside her on the mattress. "I'm glad you came. I wanted to apologize."

"That's all right. I know your heart was in the right place. Did everything go all right for you tonight?"

Delta nods yes, then we both sit there with feelings too big for this room to hold.

"Em, does the future ever scare you so much you can hardly breathe?"

"Since Mike died, every day of my life."

I'm so scared of never having that kind of relationship again I want to crawl in a hole and pull it in behind me. I'm so terrified of never having every little thing I do validated by a once-in-a-lifetime man who could convey an encyclopedia of love with one look that I'd like to curl into a corner for the rest of my life.

Delta's the wise one, the smart one, but now she's waiting, depending on me.

"You just get in a quiet place and find your center, then keep moving forward. That's all."

I take a deep breath and start searching for my center, hoping I can follow my own advice.

CHAPTER 10

Our journeys often take us to places filled with
wildlife. Animals are like people: you need
to know who you are dealing with. If you're
facing a mad moose, run.

The Seasoned Traveler's Guide to Denali,

Delta Jordan

Emily

Last night I dreamed Mike was in his boat calling
back to the shore for me to find something, but I
couldn't understand what it was. I woke up in a
panic, thinking surely it was my center and I had
lost it for good, then turned into one of those over-
eager widows so desperate for the company of a man
I'd go out with a warthog.

Not that Cliff is one.

I head to the kitchen at the crack of dawn and start cooking. By the time Delta gets up, I've cooked enough eggs for Alexander the Great's army, and Cliff has already called to invite me to drive with him to Florence, which he says is the one place in Italy everybody must see.

"I thought I smelled coffee."

In the light of day I can see a beard burn on Delta's chin, and I get so nostalgic I feel like weeping.

"If you go out with somebody twice, does that mean you're dating?"

I hand Delta a cup of coffee then sit down hard, waiting.

"No," she says, and I tell her thank you.

Still, when I call Cliff I tell him I can't go today because I promised Rosa I'd knit. Which I did. The refreshing surprise of Cliff is that he knows I'm not playing games.

Well, at my age, who would?

Oh, and did I say Rosa and I are teaching each other a few useful phrases? I can say *Mi scusi*, excuse me—which is the polite way to say everything here—*puo fare un cambio dell'olio per me?* That means, Can you change my oil? I don't know why Rosa wanted me to learn that unless she thinks I'm several quarts low.

I taught her My love is like a red, red rose, because the flower sounds like her name and I thought the phrase suited her.

Anyhow, we're making real progress here, Delta and I. My tank is slowly filling up and her running shoes are sitting under her bed, neglected.

When I leave the villa she's in the courtyard with her laptop and the slowly-inching-toward-each-other tortoises. Maybe I should take a lesson from them.

When I come back, Delta's in the hall holding another letter from Antonio on that lovely paper I've learned is handmade.

Today I bought some paper that looks marbleized and I'm going to write home to my children and let them know I've met Cliff Booth. And that I like him, but not in any way that should cause alarm.

"Em, I'm meeting Antonio at his mother's villa. She was sick and couldn't come to the opening."

"Is this relationship getting serious?"

"I'm taking the rental car, if it's all right with you."

This is typical Delta, still trying to maintain control, always prepared to run.

"Good grief, Delta. I wouldn't drive it, even if you left it here. I'd end up so lost nobody would ever find me."

"We're going to work on that before we leave."

"Go. Have fun. And, Delta, I hope this is an amazing evening for you."

"You know something, Em? So do I."

Delta

It's easy to see where Antonio got his looks. He has his mother's carved cheekbones, her patrician nose and fine-boned hands. Although Gina's smiling as she serves tea and cake from heavy, ornate silver, it's obvious she'd like to cut my head off and serve it on the platter.

Antonio's oblivious to the dark looks she sends me. What I can't figure out is why she's so hostile. I'm sitting here being careful not to cross my legs and act too casual, too American. I'm carrying on what would be considered by most people an intelligent conversation in perfectly passable Italian, and I'm wearing a conservative skirt and a blouse I've deliberately buttoned so I'm not showing everything I've got.

Which is considerable, thank you very much. I'm not some wilting waif. I'm a well-endowed woman with real hips and real breasts. Tall, granted. Certainly not fat. But not one of your flat-bellied, no-bottomed cute young things, either.

His mother stands and he offers to help her carry the tea things to the kitchen.

"No. She will come."

Gina acts as if she doesn't know my name. Not a good sign. Once we're in her kitchen, she closes the door. Another bad omen.

"Antonio will soon have a fiancée," she says. "A nice, Catholic girl."

Of course he will. A man that handsome. He'd have a fiancée plus six other women waiting in the wings.

"We're just friends."

Am I trying to convince her or myself?

"He'll have an Italian wife, lots of children."

Jerking the silver platter out of my hands, she says, "You are too old for children. My son is thirty-five. If he marries you, I will make my peace with God then stick my head in the oven."

I wasn't going to have children with him, wasn't even thinking of marriage, but all of a sudden I'm doing the math. I'm seventy with gallstones and irritable bowel while he's fifty-seven and virile. No amount of love—or sex, as the case may be—can overcome that.

Also there's the matter of two different cultures, two different countries.

"Thank you for the tea," I tell her, and then hold myself together long enough to tell Antonio that I feel sick and have to go home.

This is not a lie. I need to put on my pink high-top shoes and run until the vision of my decrepit old age and his understandable desertion clears my head. I need to come back drained of everything, including the ludicrous idea that a few magical days could grow into a summer-long love affair. And, yes, I'll admit it, a lifetime connection. Then I need to drink lots of tall beverages, preferably alcoholic, till I return to the relative sanity I enjoyed before I became the stereotype of a foolish American woman who fell under the spell of a handsome Italian artist.

Antonio wants me to lie down upstairs, to hold a wet cloth to my head, to call a doctor, to drive me home. I say no to everything and make my getaway before he discovers Gina with her head in the oven.

Back at the villa, Emily takes one look at my face and knows.

"What happened?"

"I've made a foolish mistake and I don't want to talk about it. I'm going to put on my running shoes and run for six years or until I grow a beard. Whichever comes first."

"Can I get you anything?"

"A brain transplant would be nice. If Antonio comes, I don't want to see him."

I change clothes and start running. If I ever finish this guide to Umbria, I'm leaving Italy and never coming back.

Emily

I feel like Grand Central Station. First Delta roars through like Metro North, then Antonio pulls in like the New York subway.

"I have come to apologize to Delta," he says.

What could he have possibly said to send her off in such a frenzy? Contrary to what I've been doing lately, which is sanctifying the dead; Mike was not perfect. And certainly I'm not. We had our spats. But we always worked things out.

I'm tempted not to tell him what she said. Delta's too stubborn for her own good. Any two people who have been as happy as they have ought to be able to sit down and talk.

"She's running. She said to tell you she didn't want to see you again."

"I will wait."

I think mountains being formed must look the way he does standing in the front hall, solid and immovable, determined to endure. I want to tell him I'm rooting for him but that would be disloyal to Delta, especially since I don't know the whole story.

Instead, I get him coffee, invite him to wait in a comfortable chair in the library. Then I take out my knitting and tell him I'll be seeing Florence tomorrow with Cliff.

"Delta and I are going with you."

I don't believe he knows my intractable friend. Antonio never wavers while she runs, never shows the slightest impatience, the slightest doubt.

By the time the front door opens, I've knitted a scarf that would reach to Texas and back, and Delta looks like she's been swimming the Atlantic.

"*Tu se veramente, bella,*" Antonio tells her.

I know *beautiful*, and I don't care what the rest of it means. If he'd said that to me in his melting voice with his melting eyes, I'd have thrown myself on the floor at his feet, begging.

And I know exactly for what. Which just goes to show that my recovery is either one of the fastest in the history of widowhood or Lucille was right and I've fallen under the spell of foreign devils.

CHAPTER 11

I can tell you the best restaurants to choose, the best hotels, the best modes of transportation. But I can't tell you how to deal with the people you meet along the way. There are no guidebooks for the human heart.

The Seasoned Traveler's Guide to Umbria,
A work in progress, Delta Jordan

Delta

"I'll leave you two alone," Emily says, then scuttles up the stairs.

I don't know whether to kill her or Antonio. If I hadn't used my last ounce of energy to get back up the hill to the villa, I'd take off running again and not stop till I get to France.

I'm still digesting his saying, *You are truly beautiful*, while I look like a limp dishrag, when he apologizes for his mother's behavior.

"She told you what she wanted to be true, Delta, not what *is* true."

"Don't blame your mother. I didn't leave because I thought you have another woman, Antonio. I left because what we have is impossible."

"I believe in faith, not doubt."

With his impassioned speech, Antonio could move mountains. Although I'm no mountain—at least not yet—I am almost persuaded to yield to his vision of the future.

But I'm a woman accustomed to dealing with facts, and there is no escaping math and geography. You don't change your age on a whim or move the ocean or relocate a continent.

"Sooner or later I would have discovered that this is all wrong, Antonio. Don't make it any harder than it has to be."

"It doesn't have to end, Delta."

"If I wanted a summer affair, I'd probably laugh at all this then do exactly as I pleased. But somewhere along the way, I found out I can't be merely casual with you."

"Nor I with you."

He's looking at me as if I'm something good to eat. If one of us doesn't get out of this room immediately, I won't be responsible for what I might do.

"Please, Antonio. Just leave."

Mercifully, he does, but after the door shuts behind him, I can't catch my breath or move my feet or feel my heart beating. These emotions are concrete blocks. That I can stand at all is a small mercy.

Emily comes in so quietly I almost think she's tiptoeing. There's a hushed quality to the way she looks at me, the way she skirts around me and sits on the sofa with her ankles crossed and her hands folded in her lap. This is the way people act when somebody dies.

"He's gone and that's the end of it, Emily."

I don't try to put a light spin on things, don't strive for the old "laughter through tears" medicine Emily and I know so well. She did it with me through the desertion of two husbands.

But Antonio deserves more and both of us know it. He deserves the respect of silence.

"I'll bake us a cake."

It's only when she gets up and leaves the room that I can move. I go into the courtyard and watch the tortoises Emily has said are trying to mate. They have inched about five feet farther than yesterday, but they still have almost half the length of the courtyard to cover.

"Don't bother," I tell them. "It will only break your hearts."

Emily

Naturally Delta and Antonio don't drive with us to Florence, and I don't know how I feel about this yet. On the one hand, it would have been nice to start the day knowing there would be no private moments, only sightseeing. But on the other, it's lovely to think that Cliff and I can veer off at any road we come to. We can meander at will and see what happens.

We don't wander off, though, but go directly to Florence. Or Firenze, as the sign says. And since I'm starving, as usual, we go directly to La Bussola, home of the world's best pizza, according to Cliff. Well, why not? Even I know that pizza is Italian.

I get to sit at a marble counter and watch the chef prepare the pizza, a real treat for a woman who loves the kitchen as much as I do.

"Cliff, after lunch, will you interpret while I ask him how he makes this dough?"

"I've never seen a woman get such a kick out of something so simple."

"This is my first time abroad."

Women seeking to impress would never have told him such a thing, but I want to make every minute count.

The chef won't tell me his secrets, but he kisses my hand for asking. I guess all that Italian charm is catching because the minute we get outside Cliff puts his hand on the back of my neck and sort of halfway turns me. The next thing you know I see his mouth heading toward mine.

To tell the truth, I have time to turn my head and receive a kiss on the cheek, but I don't. I kiss him right there in public like a woman who knows what she's doing and what she wants.

I had almost forgotten how this feels, a tall, strong man's arms around me, and me standing on tiptoe to reach. Feminine and desirable, that's how I feel…and awash with guilt.

I'm sorry, Mike, I'm sorry.

But Mike would have wanted me to go on living my life wide open. I know this. *After I'm gone…*he'd say, but I would tell him to hush up, who was to say he'd die first. I could be incubating some terrible disease even as we spoke.

Now here I am kissing another man so soon, *so soon*, and not just any man, but my old flame, who is not nearly as handsome as Mike, but who is—in a rugged way—sexy and good-looking as all get out. I'm feeling excited but wretched and horrible and unworthy to still be wearing Mike's ring.

I can tell you one thing, for sure—I would be rolling in my grave if Mike so much as looked at another woman after my death. I'd die all over again at the idea that some brazen heifer would stick her tacky clothes in my closet and parade her skinny self around naked in front of my husband. *Mine*. Forever and always.

Somebody ought to cart me off to the loony bin.

"Emily," Cliff is saying to me now. "I'm sorry. Did I embarrass you?"

"Well, not exactly. I liked it."

"Good, I'm thinking about doing it again."

"Not just yet. I'm not ready."

"When do you think you will be."

"I don't know. Maybe in six years. Or maybe tomorrow."

"I like you, Emily Jordan."

"Jones."

"Whatever your name is. Maybe I'll just call you Babe."

"You do and you'll be sporting a black eye."

We're laughing as we head up the hill to see Michelangelo's *David*, and it feels almost as good as a kiss. And much, much safer.

Delta

While Emily's in Florence, another letter comes from Antonio. Although I'm tempted not to open it, I haven't yet become a complete coward.

Dear Delta,

I would come to your villa today and stay until
I convince you that only the kindest of fates
could have brought us together, only the wisest
of gods could have foreseen the magic we knew.

But I must return to my home on the *lago*
of Piediliuco to prepare for an art exhibition
in Rome. I will be there the remainder of
the summer.

Although I want to send flowers and gifts
and passionate pleas to make you change your
mind, I will not disrespect you with such an
outrageous display of affection. I will, how-
ever, continue to write so that you can know I
have not forgotten you. I will never forget you.
Yours,
Antonio

This letter sends me racing up Mount Subasio in
my high-top sneakers. I don't come down until it's
almost dark and time for Emily to be home.

When she's not there, I wait at the window,

straining my eyes into the distance and the darkness for the first signs of her. That she's not late enough to make me worry is another of the universe's small mercies.

"Emily, I've finished my research in the Assisi area, and I can't be here anymore."

I can't stay in this villa and watch letters arrive from a man I want but can't have.

"I know."

She puts her arms around me, and I wish I were a child again, a six-year-old who could lean into her while she whispers, "Everything's going to be all right."

I straighten up and try to get control of my ragged emotions.

"Some of the small towns in Umbria are more than a day trip away," I tell her. "I'm leaving tomorrow, and will stay till I finish my research, probably another two weeks. I'd love to have you with me, or you can stay here."

"I hate for you to be alone, Delta, but Cliff's going to be here another week." I wave my hand, dismissing her worries. "I'd really like to spend some more time with him, see what happens."

Emily's dressed in yellow, a color that suits her cheerful mood. Cliff is coming for lunch then she's taking him to meet Rosa. I hug her hard and say, "You be good."

"Ha."

If I didn't know her better I'd be afraid to leave her alone, scared she'd do something foolish. But Emily has always been a kidder. She always likes to keep you guessing...and keep you laughing. Lately I've seen how she's beginning to take charge of her own life, so I leave without the least qualm that she will get herself into a situation she can't handle.

The truth is, I can travel faster without her, and the sooner I finish my job and get out of this country, the better I'll be.

As I turn the rental car north toward Gubbio, I'm very much aware that the road to Lake Piediliuco leads south. By the time I have to circle back to

Terni and Todi, Arrone and Polino, Antonio will be in Rome.

And I'll be safe.

CHAPTER 12

Expect the unexpected in Umbria. It's a land
of magic and surprise.

The Seasoned Traveler's Guide to Umbria,
A work in progress, Delta Jordan

Emily

When Delta pulls out of the driveway I get an
insane urge to run along behind the rental car and
yell "Wait for me." The only thing that stops me is
the yellow dress. It's a hot, dry day and I don't want
to get road dust all over it and mess it up, which just
goes to show that no matter how far I've come I'm
still the same frivolous woman at heart.

Oh, well, I never set out to turn myself into something I'm not, just to change a few of my baser habits.

When the doorbell rings I jump as if I'm shot. Cliff's standing in the sunshine with a bouquet of fresh daisies.

"These made me think of you, Em." He pecks me on the cheek. "You look nice in yellow."

The last time I wore yellow for Mike was six weeks into his illness when both of us thought nothing could change our lives. *You're delicious*, he said, then grabbed me around the waist and waltzed me to the bedroom where he proceeded to taste me all over, just to prove his point.

All of a sudden I miss him so much I want to climb up the wall backward and beat my fists against the ceiling. Or is it intimacy I miss? Or both?

Well, here's the perfect opportunity to change that. An empty villa, a big inviting bed, a willing man and all the time in the world.

Come upstairs, I can say. *Let's play.*

"Em, it's early. Do you want to eat first or visit your friend Rosa?"

If I don't get out of this house I'll not be responsible for what I might do.

"Visit Rosa."

I grab a sun hat and a loaf of cranberry bread I made as a gift.

"You're going to love her and she's going to love you," I tell Cliff, which turns out to be exactly the opposite of the truth.

I can tell this right off the bat, even though I don't understand a word she's saying unless it's about excusing me and changing my oil. Everything Rosa thinks about Cliff is in her body language; stiff, unyielding posture and thunderous expression.

They're exchanging a rapid-fire conversation and the only thing I can make out, so far, is *serpente*.

Good grief, either a snake's going to bite me or she's just called Cliff a snake.

"Do you want to leave?" I ask him, and he waves the question aside, laughing.

"I haven't had this much fun since my high school baseball coach chewed me out for allowing three runs in the ninth inning."

"That was *fun?*"

"It was a challenge. Not too many people challenge me."

"Do I?"

"If you didn't, I wouldn't be hanging around."

"Tell Rosa you're my good friend, and she should make an effort to be nice to you."

I watch this exchange. "She said you should be more careful choosing your friends. You should find a handsome man and not one whose jaw looks like a shovel."

"Tell her if she'll apologize, she can have the cranberry bread."

Rosa grins at the mention of a gift.

"She said that old women are entitled to their opinions, but she's sorry she upset you and she's happy to accept your peace offering."

After we leave Rosa with her bribe, Cliff suggests we have lunch in Assisi since we're already there. I decide the spirit of Saint Francis, which permeates this town, must be watching over me because I'm much too vulnerable to be trusted alone with this man in Delta's rented villa. And the last thing I need to do is take a flying leap backward after I've come so far.

Delta

Here is what I'm writing: "Surrounded by wooded hills and mountains, the Lake Piediluco is the second largest in Umbria."

Here is what I'm feeling: excited and scared, hopeful and regretful.

Finally I'm in the place where Antonio lives. Although I know he's in Rome and I'm safe from a chance encounter, I feel his presence everywhere. But most of all I feel him in the large villa that hugs the lake and sits behind a wrought-iron fence whose centerpiece is a D in Old English script. Donacelli.

Although I simply *knew*, I asked, just to be certain.

Taking out my cell phone, I call Em.

"How are you making out without me?" I ask.

"The day after you left I tried to buy apples at the market and ended up with asparagus. The way the vendor was laughing I think I must have asked to buy the old man sitting beside her in a straw hat. What about you?"

"I'm standing in front of Antonio's house feeling like the world's biggest fool."

"I don't know why."

"Because I don't know if he's the best thing that ever happened to me or the worst."

"Aw, Delta. Quit being so hard on yourself. Everything in this life doesn't come with a travel guide."

"It ought to."

"Then you'd miss all the surprises."

I don't think I want to be surprised anymore. It hurts too much.

I tell Em I'll be back in a couple of days and then I drive away. Over the years I've perfected the skill of not looking back. At times like this, my gratitude for this small armor is infinite.

Emily

I'm standing here in the little grocery store on the piazza saying, *Quanto costa?* which means How much? no matter what you're talking about. I don't have to know the words for chicken and eggplant and bread and cheese. All I have to do is say those two words and count out my money.

Oh, and watch the shopkeepers giggle at Italian spoken badly with a Southern accent.

That's one good thing about being on my own for the past week: I'm learning to fend for myself. The other is that I have the villa all to myself to do exactly as I please. And tonight it pleases me to have Cliff come to dinner.

He brings wine, and when we sit down and start talking with the ease of an old married couple, I remember that I was going to marry Cliff and have four boys and teach piano while he coached baseball. But Daddy had other ideas because Cliff was from the wrong side of the tracks, a brash boy who would never amount to a hill of beans. Daddy's exact words.

And so Cliff took his football scholarship to Alabama where he became part of the Crimson Tide. In record time he had rolled over the competition and Bitsy Wheeler, to boot. The cheerleader who, according to his sister, followed him to Alabama and snagged him on the rebound.

From me, who is refilling my glass and feeling

sixteen. Who never played rockabilly music at the Baptist church because her husband had the gall to die first.

I'm very much alive and hungry and maybe a little bit tipsy because I reach over with my fork and take a bite out of Cliff's plate, something I always did with my husband, who thought it was cute.

I guess Cliff does, too, because he lifts his glass and I click mine against it. He's smiling as big as jackasses eating sawbriars, and I guess I am, too, because my mouth feels stretched and funny and so does my stomach.

"I think I have to go to the toilet."

That didn't come out right. I meant to say "powder my nose," which is what Southern ladies of breeding and good taste—also a certain age—say to hide their true intentions.

But my true intentions seem intent on doing me in because I lurch sideways and land in Cliff's lap, and it feels so good I wallow there a minute.

Then my stomach lurches again and he untangles me, sets me upright and points me in the direction of the downstairs bathroom.

I am drunk. I grab hold of the spinning toilet and hang on, while Cliff knocks on the door and asks if I'm all right.

"I don't know," I tell him, which is the absolute truth about everything, the state of my stomach, the state of my mind, the state of my heart. Even the state of Texas where Lucille would be spitting tornadoes if she knew what I have on my mind tonight.

Had. Still have. Lord help me, I don't know that, either.

Cliff comes into the bathroom and wipes my face with wet toilet paper because I forgot to hang a hand towel yesterday and he can't find the storage cabinet.

When I stand upright and see myself in the mirror above the sink, I look like some pitiful, molting bird, a blob of toilet paper stuck to my chin and bits of it clinging to my sticking-out hair.

"This is my fault, Emily. I forgot you never did have a head for alcohol."

Somebody ought to reward him with a small country.

"I'd better get you upstairs."

That sounds like a wonderful idea until we get into the bedroom and he starts unbuttoning my blouse. I don't think he's noticed the toilet paper, and if he has, he doesn't care.

And I don't think he means to tuck me in bed and turn out the light and leave me here by myself to sleep this off, though I know he would never take advantage of my tipsy state to do anything I didn't want.

What I want is for my life to go back to the way it was before Mike's cancer. What I want is to feel like a woman and not feel guilty.

What I get is a messy bunch of feelings I can't deal with and Cliff Booth with a gleam in his eye as he concentrates on the tiny pearl buttons.

The part of me that's deprived and restless wants to help him. But the part of me that remembers other hands on my blouse, other legs entwined with mine, suddenly feels like an onion, layers of grief and fear topped by a thick covering of remorse.

"Stop. Please."

He backs off instantly. "Do you want to go back downstairs?"

I nod. Anywhere is better than here. Where I made a complete fool of myself. Where I pretended

I have never made vows that included till death do us part. What I'd meant to say was, Forever and ever, but take me first because I don't want to be the one left behind.

We start down the stairs, but I'm wobbly inside and out. How can I make small talk after this?

"I've changed my mind. I just want to go to bed. By myself. I'm sorry I ruined your last night in Italy."

"Good Lord, Emily. You haven't ruined anything. I've had a great time." He kisses my cheek. "See you in the U.S.A."

I climb into bed, grateful for the sheet. Grateful I can pull it over my head and hide so I won't have to see the moon and stars pouring light through the window, so I won't have to feel it on my skin in a way that reminds me of Mike lying beside me.

"You are beautiful in the moonlight," he said. Even when I wasn't. Even when I knew he knew I wasn't.

If I weren't afraid of toppling down the stairs, I'd get the rest of the wine, lie in bed and drink it through a straw till the whole bottle is gone. Then I wouldn't have to worry about sex when your partner's gone or Thanksgiving turkey for one or how to untangle Christmas lights and what to do if one on the string goes bad and they all go out.

I think I'll have a bologna sandwich instead of a turkey and I don't think I'll put up lights this year. I think I'm going to live in this bed for the rest of my life and view the outside world from this tall window. And then only when it's pitch-dark.

I'm a basket case, and the only good thing I can say about myself is that my basket is not quite as big as it was before I came to Italy.

I don't know who turned loose a herd of elephants at my front door, but if I ever get down this staircase without breaking my neck, I'm going to shoot somebody.

"Em? Good grief, what happened to you?"

"I got drunk last night and threw myself at Cliff then learned he was too much of a gentleman to take advantage of me. You don't look so hot yourself."

"I'm ready to pack and go home."

"You'll probably want to open these first."

I hand her a thick stack of letters that have collected on the hall table, every one of them from

Antonio. She shoves them into her briefcase without even looking.

"I think you should open them."

"What's the use? I knew from the beginning it wouldn't work out."

"You knew no such thing. He's a great guy and you're just being bullheaded. At least see what he has to say."

"No. Nothing's more ridiculous than a woman who turns herself into a cliché."

If my head didn't feel like an overripe watermelon, I'd argue till I wore her down and she'd open the letters just to get me to shut up. As it is, I totter into the kitchen and make coffee strong enough to jumpstart the dead, then sit at the table and say thank you. Just that.

I don't have to go into any long-winded explanations. God can look into my junkyard mind and my bombed-out, under-reconstruction heart and know exactly what I mean.

CHAPTER 13

Umbria is a land magically transported out
of time, a land of medieval and Renaissance
influences that make it easy to forget who you
are and why you came.

The Seasoned Traveler's Guide to Umbria,
A work in progress, Delta Jordan

Emily

I'm carrying home enough knitted goods to slip-
cover Texas while Delta's carrying home Antonio's
letters, which I take as a very positive sign.

After she got back from her whirlwind data-
gathering tour and I got over my hangover, I nagged
her some more, but it didn't do a lick of good. I'm
hoping she'll change her mind when we get back to
the States.

High over the Atlantic I wonder if he'll keep writing and what he'll do when his letters start coming back marked Return to Sender. He could find her, of course, through Cliff, but I've always thought of his letters as a bubble bath for the spirit. I've always thought he knew something about romance that most men that young never grasp— the beauty and power of the written word.

I wonder what Delta will do if he finds her. More to the point, I wonder what she'll do if he doesn't. If nobody does.

Maybe I'll talk to Mike about this when I get home. Go down to the lake and see if I can connect with his spirit again, see if he can give me some good, otherwordly guidance about how to help my friend.

Of maybe I'll just call Cliff and say, "Look, if Antonio is serious, tell him to get his gorgeous butt over here and make Delta believe in love again."

More importantly, make her believe in herself. She did, briefly, in our sun-struck Italian summer.

This time I wanted to sit in the window seat, and now I see the first sight of land.

"Look, Delta."

"Are you glad you went, Em?"

"Yes. Thanks to you and the sunflower fields and Rosa and about fifty skeins of good yarn I'm now focused on *la dolce vita*."

"Been practicing Italian, have you?"

"No. I saw the movie. When I get back to the States, I'm having the sweet life, no matter who pitches a hissy fit."

"I'll be looking for a place of my own."

"You don't have to move."

"Now that I know you're going to be all right, yes, I do."

"At least stay till the family reunion."

"The Jones family?" When I nod, she says, "I know you're doing great, but are you sure you're up to entertaining that big crowd?"

That's the same question I asked Mike the year before he died, but he said, "We always have it and this year is going to be no different." Then he sat in his wheelchair on the deck, his chemo-induced baldness covered with a Mississippi State baseball cap, and laughed the loudest when Brennan set the hamburgers on fire and Lucille tried to put them out with lemonade. He was wise that way, enjoying every moment of life as long as he could.

I miss all that, his laughter, his wisdom, his love, but now I'm just going to have to make some different memories.

First, though, I have to get home and figure out where I'm going to put enough knitted goods to stuff a small baby elephant.

I call down the hall where Delta's unpacking.

"Do you want to drive into town and get hamburgers tonight?"

"No. As soon as I finish here I'm going to work. The sooner I get through with this book the better."

What she's not saying is that she wants to forget about Italy, forget about Antonio, forget that for a few weeks she let every one of her feelings show.

Delta has stuck by me for months. I'm not fixing to leave her be alone when she's the one in need.

"Okay," I say. "I don't think I'll go either. I'm too tired."

I take the last of Laura's lemon pies out of the freezer, zap it in the microwave then eat standing up. But I eat only one piece, and not once do I feel the need to eat the whole pie.

Then I call Cliff, who happens to be very glad to hear from me, and who also happens to get the wrong idea.

"Listen, Cliff. Forget that last night in Italy. Everybody ought to be entitled to pitch a drunk and act insane every once in a while."

"It was fun. Sort of like reliving our high school days. I'd like to see you again, Emily."

What seemed so easy in a place far removed from your real life suddenly seems like something you ought to sit down and think twice about. Dating. There's a protocol for widows in the South, and while I've never been one to abide by anybody's rules, I do care about my reputation.

Lord, I sound like Lucille.

"Listen, Cliff, not just yet. Okay? Anyhow, that's not why I called you."

Now that I've leaped before looking, I can't bring myself to enlist his help in patching things up between Delta and Antonio. It feels too much like a betrayal of my best friend. Who do I think I am, a woman who just recently patched up her own falling-apart life?

"I just wanted to thank you for showing me around Italy."

I feel like a better person when I go to bed, a woman finally taking charge of my own life. Even though my overstuffed suitcases are still lined up in the hall, I don't know diddly-squat about Mike's business and I'll have to build a wing on the house if I keep buying yarn.

Delta

The pounding on the front door wakes me up and there stands Buddy Earl with Emily's mean cat. He ogles me as if I'm naked instead of standing here in a nightshirt barely long enough to cover all my major body parts and sporting a slogan proclaiming, Support Wildlife. Throw a Party.

"I like your outfit, Delta."

I'm going to burn it. I'm going to stop wearing

these clothes that declare things I'll never do. Where's my robe when I need it? Where's Emily?

Crashed and burned, probably, the same way I was till Buddy Earl's racket woke me. I'd never have gone to the door half-naked if I hadn't been so jet-lagged.

"Thanks for bringing the cat home." Leo streaks past me and heads straight to Emily's bedroom.

"Now that you're back, maybe the two of us can go bowling or something, maybe make some bologna sandwiches and have a picnic down by the lake."

The last time I was on a lake I got into big trouble. Not that I have any desire to go anywhere with Buddy Earl. Still, Italy turned loose a river of new feelings in me. Instead of seeing Howdy Doody in a cowboy hat, I see a man trying to fill up some of his loneliness.

"Thank you, Buddy Earl. I really appreciate your invitation, but I'm too busy to go out."

He looks so dejected when he leaves I want to run along behind him and give advice, tell him to invite the nice divorcée down the street on a date or join a singles group. I'm good at that. What I'm not good at is taking it.

The bass greeting of an air horn shifts my attention to a barge on the waterway, and I'm jerked backward to Italy, to the day on a lake where everything seemed possible.

From now on, maybe I'll stick to travel guides within the continental U.S. That way I won't have to contend with jet lag and foreign charmers with talented hands and a mother who hates me.

When I go back into my bedroom, the first thing I see is Antonio's letters stacked in a box on the dresser. I should burn them but I can't. While I'm shoving the box under the bed, I hear a commotion in Emily's room that sounds as if she'd herding Texas longhorns.

Boxes are everywhere—stacked beside her suitcase, spilling out of Mike's closet, shoved under the bed. Emily's dragging one across the floor, leaving a trail of brightly colored yarn. Actually she's dragging Leo, too, because his claws are snagged in the yarn, and if that defiant posture is any signal, he has no intention of letting go.

"Em, what in the world are you doing?"

"I was sleeping till Buddy Earl brought Leo home. Now I'm trying to fit all this somewhere."

"If Mike's closet were empty, it would hold everything."

"No."

"It was just a suggestion, not a criticism. I won't mention it again."

"If you do, I'm liable to stick my head in the oven."

"I can't believe you said that, Em."

"Well, Mike's dead and Antonio's in Italy. Let's just both stick our heads in the oven."

All of a sudden I see the humor of it, the rich wisdom. I can become a woman who resorts to histrionics or I can learn to laugh at myself, to take myself lightly. Women weighed down by trouble can't fly.

I smile and Emily giggles, then we start laughing and can't stop. I picture us growing old this way, best friends sitting in side-by-side rocking chairs at the rest home, laughing at every little thing.

"Seriously, Em, what are you going to do with all those afghans and scarves you knitted?"

"Put mothballs around them?"

"Wait a minute. I just had a thought. I want to show you something."

I log onto the Internet and pull up the Project Linus Web site. I watch while Emily reads how women across the U.S. are knitting, quilting and crocheting for newborns who come into this world without parents who stick around or blankets to cover their little naked bodies.

She goes from a tearful "Oh, my" to an excited "Oh, my gosh."

"I can do this," she finally says. "I can start a Linus chapter. I can build a meeting place with a storage warehouse. Heck, I can hire people to help, if that's what it takes. Oh, Lord, Delta."

I know what she's saying. Emily, who views herself as helpless and frivolous, who thought her life was over when Mike died, who thinks her only purpose on this earth is to cook wonderful meals and make people laugh at parties, *this* Emily has discovered a way to stand on her own, to make her life count.

We print out everything we can find on Project Linus. Then she races back to her bedroom and starts sorting her blankets while I hole up with my computer and try to turn my notes into a guidebook instead of a painful reminder of what I found, then lost, in Italy.

Emily

When Delta was finishing her guide to spas she'd sit at her computer and type so fast it sounded like machine-gun fire coming from the basement. Now she's down there trying to finish her guidebook to Italy, and I hear sporadic bursts of typing followed by long lulls. This has been going on for five days, and I can't sit back and keep quiet one minute longer.

I carry a plate of chocolate chip cookies and two cups of Green Tea Chai down the stairs.

"Coffee break," I say.

Sometimes chocolate works miracles. I wait for this to happen, but I don't see a single bit of tension leaving her face, even after three cookies.

"Call him, Delta."

"No. Even if it had been real instead of some kind of joke, it was never going to work out. The age factor, alone, was enough to destroy any chances I might have had with Antonio."

"It didn't seem to bother him."

"I'm fairly well preserved. He didn't know."

"For Pete's sake, you make yourself sound like a

jar of pickles. Get off your pity pot and drive into town with me. I'm meeting Glenda Noles, the new business manager in John's office, then I'm buying two tons of groceries for the Jones family reunion."

"Okay. I could use a break." She turns off the computer and follows me up the stairs. "I'm driving."

Sometimes I think Delta reads minds. She knows I'm worried about meeting this woman who is going to whip me and my business into shape. When my mind's on other things I don't drive worth a toot.

When we walk into John's office and see Glenda, my worst fears are confirmed. She looks like Godzilla in high heels, the type of woman who would gladly twist your head off if you disagreed with her.

I feel every inch the dumpy, unprepared, scatter-brained woman I am. Thank God I have Delta with me. She can hold her own against anybody.

Perching on the edge of my chair while John explains Glenda's credentials—business degrees from Boston College and Columbia, business management with the Chrysler Corporation and IBM—I hang on to my purse and try to look efficient. Or at least, moderately intelligent.

I wish I were knitting. I wish I were baking a peach pie. I wish I were anywhere except in a business office where I don't even know the right questions to ask. Let alone any answers.

Glenda leans toward me, her belly fat folding over like yeast-rising rolls.

"I'm not nearly as mean as I look nor as intimidating as John makes me sound," she says. "Furthermore, I'm going to talk to you in layman's terms so you and I can make decisions about your business together."

Not Mike's business. *Mine*. All of a sudden I see how it's going to be with the two of us. Her leaning on my kitchen cabinet licking the icing bowl while I stir the cookie dough and tell her exactly how big I want the building for the Linus Project.

"Thank you," I tell her.

Then I say thank you to the universe. Every day I see another example of grace.

CHAPTER 14

The miracle of Assisi is not that St. Francis
received the stigmata and communicated with
animals so many years ago, but that the place
can still lift the spirit and transform the heart
and soul.

The Seasoned Traveler's Guide to Umbria,
A work in progress, Delta Jordan

Emily

When we get home there's a truck with a Texas
tag in the driveway. Oh Lord, Lucille.

She bails out of the truck before Delta can get the
car parked.

"I thought I'd better come on up early and help

you get ready for the reunion. Where've you been? I nearly roasted to death in my truck."

"Hello to you, too, Lucille. Why didn't you wait on the deck where it's cool?"

"I'm not one to go poking around where I don't belong. Let me just stow my bags, then I'll get these boxes out of the car and we'll start loading up Mike's things."

Leo streaks around the corner, hissing. Next he leaps into a pot of basil and tears it to shreds then climbs a tree to find a safe perch. I wish I were a cat. I'd hiss and run, too. There she stands with her Coke bottle lenses, her sturdy Nikes and her Buster Brown haircut, looking like a beetle-browed nurse carrying castor oil in her carpetbag purse.

"If by 'things' you mean his clothes, I'm not ready to do that yet, and that's my decision to make."

Well, I'm proud of myself. Before I went to Italy I'd have helped her box them up, hauled them off in the trunk of my car, pretended I dumped them then put them back after she left. So that's progress, I think.

But if I'm so far advanced along this healing path, why can't I give the clothes to a needy person?

"I got up at the crack of dawn to get here. The least I expect is a little appreciation."

Oh, Lord, Mike. How am I going to handle this sister of yours without you to straighten out the misunderstandings?

Delta's still in the driveway, and if I looked at her a certain way she'd step in and take charge.

Instead I put my arm around Lucille's shoulder and lead her into the house.

"Come in and have some pie and coffee, Lucille." Getting her into the house is as difficult as catching the granddaddy of all catfish in the waterway. Mike tried for years, but the closest he ever got was snagging it and losing his bait.

I finally get her mind off taking charge of my life by asking her to tell me stories of Mike's childhood. She's known—and loved—him far longer than I, and we settle down to an evening of reminiscences.

I can do this, I can enjoy being with this Lucille. Getting the family photograph album, we flip through the pages while Delta unloads the groceries.

"Who is that?" Lucille points to a photograph of a tall man and a woman with exquisite cheekbones.

"Delta's parents."

Delta drops a loaf of bread, then picks it up as if nothing has happened. But I see the look on her face, as if she's standing in front of a pet store and doesn't even have enough money for a leash, let alone a dog.

After Lucille goes to bed, I say, "Delta, you need to find your father."

"No. And that's the end of it." She marches off, stiff-backed and disappears into the basement. In a minute she'll be burning up the computer keys, escaping without her high-top running shoes.

Lord, this kind of stubbornness makes me hungry. I get some Ritz crackers then discover I've forgotten to buy cheese. Tomorrow I'll send Lucille to Wal-Mart to get some. That ought to give her a sense of purpose. I rummage in the bottom drawer of the refrigerator until I find a piece of cheddar that hasn't died and gone to heaven, and then I go onto the deck and watch the movement of moonlight on the water until my skin fits me again.

"Thank you," I say. Just that. Thank you.

Delta

The next day I'm at the family reunion eating pie and drinking iced tea and listening to Michele and her husband Davis, both doctors, advising their great-aunt Gertrude and uncle Simpson about acid reflux. I don't want to be here. I don't want to hear Lucille telling about the Christmas she dressed up like Santa Claus and Grandpa Jones's pipe set her beard on fire.

Even if I had grown up in the bosom of a loving, two-parent family that created marvelous special memories—which I definitely did not—being in the midst of somebody else's family tradition would still make me, like any single woman, feel completely alone. Besides, Antonio had a large family...and beautiful hands and the promise of an impossible future.

Suddenly my feelings are too big for my skin.

"I'm going for a drive," I tell Emily.

As I head to my Jeep Liberty I pull out my cell phone and dial my editor's number. When she answers I feel grounded, fully connected to a life I know and understand.

"I'm going to be about two weeks late delivering *The Seasoned Traveler's Guide to Umbria*."

A first for me. I don't tell her why. I don't say, "Reading my notes makes me weep." Instead I climb into the Jeep and shut the door.

"Delta."

Good grief! Who is tapping on my window but Cliff Booth?

"I drove over to visit my sister and thought I'd surprise Emily. Looks like she's having a little party."

"Family reunion."

"Good. I'll get to meet her family."

"This might not be the best time, Cliff," I tell him. "This is Mike's family. Why don't you wait here while I get Emily?"

Thank goodness he does. I go inside, motion to Emily and give her the news.

"Do you want me to tell him to leave and come back in a couple of days when the coast is clear?"

"For Pete's sake, Delta. That would be just plain rude."

Emily

I'm not as brave as I sound, but if I'm going to live my own life, I might as well start now. Putting my hand through Cliff's arm, I take him inside with Delta trailing along behind. Riding shotgun. Thank God.

Wouldn't you know it? The first person to spot us is Lucille. She trots toward us in that swagger that makes her look as if she's toting six-shooters. And maybe she is. She's probably got a couple stashed in her purse.

"Lucille, I'd like you to meet my friend, Cliff Booth."

"Who's he? Is he kin?"

"No, he's an old friend. From high school days. From before I met Mike."

"An old boyfriend? What's he doing in my brother's house?"

You can hear her bray all the way to Texas. It brings Michele running. She's like her daddy, far too brainy and sensible to panic, and yet here she comes, her lovely forehead wrinkled in concern, her blond hair streaming behind her like wings.

"Wait here," I tell Cliff, then head my daughter off at the pass. My Lord, I feel like the sheriff in an old shoot-'em-up Western movie.

"Michele, don't make a scene."

"I want to meet him, that's all."

"He's not a boyfriend, Michele. Just a friend."

"Either way, Mother. It's all right. Just let me catch my breath a minute."

She stands perfectly still, this caring, intelligent daughter so much like her father. I watch while she gets her feelings under control, then she nods, smiles and we start toward Cliff, our arms linked.

Now, where is Lucille? While I'm introducing Michele, I find out. Brennan's steaming this way like the *Titanic* with that little bow-legged tattle-tale trotting along behind. My son dwarfs Cliff by a good three inches, has the size of a linebacker and the ferocious, cock-sure look of a young male leader of a lion pride. He would look formidable if it weren't for his cowlick.

"If I had my horse whip, I'd whip you all the way back to Texas," Lucille shouts at Cliff.

Brennan restrains her with his big hand on her

arm. "Now, Aunt Lucille, let's find out his motives, first."

Aunt Gertrude is shouting, "What did they say?" while Uncle Simpson says, "I think they're talking about taking a locomotive to Disney."

I'd like to upend the pitcher of cold lemonade over Lucille's head.

"Now hear this." At five feet and four inches, I'm not a very commanding woman, but my children tell me that when I get mad I'm about ten feet tall. "This is my house, and everybody who can't behave can hit the door. Right now."

Delta presides over the uneasy peace at the grill while I'm mopping up lemonade I spilled. Aunt Gertrude and Uncle Simpson still think we're going to Disney on a locomotive, Michele and Brennan finally got Lucille to calm down and Cliff left for his sister's.

"Next time, please call," I told him, and he got the picture. We don't know each other well enough for surprises of that kind. And I don't know if I want to. After today, I doubt that he does, either.

All I know is that I *am* going to live my own life, no matter who pouts about it.

Delta slides through the door along with a blast of rock 'n' roll from Brennan's boom box.

"Everything all right in here?"

"We could stick our heads in the oven or we could dance."

Delta grabs a broom and we shimmy with our stick partners for all we're worth, then collapse on the sofa.

"I'll say this for you, Em. You certainly know how to throw a family reunion."

"Another tradition bites the dust."

"Oh, I don't know. Anything could happen in a year."

"Keep telling yourself that, Delta."

She jumps up as if I've stung her with a cattle prod.

"Don't you even want to *know* about Antonio?"

"No. It's over."

"If it's over, why are you so upset?"

"My Lord, Emily, you just had World War Three in here. That's enough to upset anybody. Let's eat."

"Do I need to wave a white flag before I go out there?"

"I think Lucille's still on the warpath."

"What else is new?"

Thank goodness Mike got the sweet genes in his family. I prance through the door as if I own the place. Which I do. Mike's gone, I'm here, I have to keep telling myself.

Delta

Emily's still sleeping, and I tiptoe into the kitchen, put on the coffee, then walk to the end of the driveway and get the paper. I'll sit on the deck while I read, sip a cup of coffee, enjoy a quiet morning. I've missed this. It's time to find my own place.

After watching how Emily handled her family's leave-taking the day after the family cookout, I'm certain she'll be okay by herself. Lucille left in high dudgeon, but Emily's children showed their fine up-bringing by taking her aside and saying they just wanted her to be happy.

I put the paper on the wrought-iron table on the deck, then go inside and add hazelnut creamer and two teaspoons of sugar to my coffee. Then I bypass world events—all that shock and trauma—and go directly to section four, arts and entertainment.

World-Renowned Artist Coming to Tupelo, the headlines scream. I know without looking, but I look anyway. Antonio Donatelli. Coming September 30. Two weeks.

Inside, the phone rings. Is it him? Calling for me? Oh, help.

Emily walks barefoot onto the deck, wearing that old blue robe. "That was Cliff. He wants to come over and apologize. Again. I'm fixing lunch. Chicken salad and maybe some of those quick brownies or a pear pie."

How can I talk about chicken salad when I can't even catch my breath?

"Delta?" She reads over my shoulder, puts her hand there and squeezes.

"He's just showing his paintings," I say. Atlanta, Chicago, New York, Boston, San Franciso and *Tupelo?*

"Wear green to the opening. It brings out the highlights in your hair."

"It's not my hair I'm worried about."

"I know." Emily sits beside me, props her feet on the table and shades her eyes as eagles soar from across the lake to an aerie that looks too big for the remnant of cypress that holds it aloft.

"They keep adding to that nest year after year. One spring lightning struck and it all fell into the water and floated down the river. But they built it right back."

I think that kind of moving forward is called faith, the kind that lets the eagles rebuild from ruins, the kind that lets Emily step onto a plane even though she was afraid it would crash.

By acting like a seasoned traveler, she became one. It seems so simple, really, the idea that we make a thing real by acting as if it's already true. But going outside our comfort zone is one of the hardest things we do, and maybe it takes more than courage, more than faith. Maybe it takes hubris, and at the moment, that's in short supply.

Emily

I'm not as smart as Delta, and I don't pretend to understand a lot of things, but I do know that she's afraid to let herself believe in love. She's afraid to let herself believe that it could happen to her because nothing in her past supports the theory that Antonio came all the way from Italy for the express purpose of seeing her—forget that he's showing his paintings and probably will visit Cliff and other friends in every major city of the U.S.

Not that I know this for a fact. I just know it on a gut level, and sometimes our gut instinct is the smartest voice we'll hear.

I'm chopping chicken for a salad made with pecans, celery, grapes and equal parts sour cream and mayonnaise, plus a good dollop of sugar, and I'm listening to my gut and I'm listening hard. What it's saying is that I should talk really straight to Delta about Antonio, but it's also saying stuff about Cliff, too, because he's my immediate concern.

I finish the chicken salad, shove it in the refrigerator and start with the pear pie. "Cliff," I'll say when he gets here, "I'd like to get to know you again and see where it goes, but I'll be darned if I'm going to be Miss Emily Easy. Just because I was once going to marry you and have your children doesn't mean I want to do anything with you now except talk about the weather.

"Furthermore," I'll tell him, "I'm a woman on the brink of discovering myself, and I'm not fixing to fall back into being the woman I was, a woman who turned herself into whatever the people around her wanted her to be."

It's a great speech, worthy of an Academy Award. Maybe even the Pulitzer.

Delta comes up the stairs where she's been tapping away at her guide to Umbria. Steadily, I might add. It's as if finding out Antonio's coming has turned loose a river inside her, and she's swimming as hard as she can to get out of the current.

"Anything I can do, Em?"

"Yeah, you need to start swimming with the current instead of against it."

"What's that supposed to mean?"

"When you see Antonio, this time go with the flow."

Delta rolls her eyes and starts arranging lettuce on the plates. I don't give a hoot whether I'm being trite or not. At least she got my point.

I'm getting ready to hammer it into her hard head when the doorbell rings. Cliff's jutted-out jaw and the flowers he holds in his hand are clearly silhouetted through the glass panel in the door, and here I stand in my blue housecoat and my bare feet, not a smidge of makeup to cover my wrinkles.

"Do you want me to entertain him while you dress?"

"Absolutely not. What he sees is what he gets."

I fling open the door. "You're early. I'm still making lunch."

"Good. I'll help."

He pecks me on the cheek, hands me daisies, strolls across the kitchen, says, "Hello, Delta," then starts chopping cucumbers and radishes.

"By the way, Em, I like the way you look. I like my women real."

"I'm not your woman and I never will be. From now on, I'm my own woman and I can guarantee I'm real."

Cliff roars with laughter and Delta smiles, which means, maybe, that she's breathing a sigh of relief and saying to herself, *Okay, now I can get on with my own life*.

I hope so. I'm going to tell her it's high time for her to quit worrying about me and start taking care of herself. I want her to give herself a chance with Antonio. But most of all I want her to dance the way we did in the sunflower fields of Italy, a dance that had nothing to do with discovering the beauty of a foreign country and everything to do with discovering the beauty inside ourselves.

But first, I want to get to know Cliff Booth, not as a girl of sixteen but as a woman rebuilding her life.

CHAPTER 15

We revisit places for all kinds of reasons. Sometimes they are as we remember, and sometimes they have changed beyond recognition.

The Seasoned Traveler's Guide to Memphis,
Delta Jordan

Delta

Cliff came back this evening to take Emily to the movies, and I'm in a house that feels too empty and too big. Echoes of the life Mike and Emily lived are everywhere, in the Mississippi State Bulldog memorabilia, in the coat closet where my raincoat is hung between his rain slicker and her poncho, in the photographs of family vacations that line the wall beside the front door.

Although it's starting to sprinkle I slip into my raincoat and head toward the road that meanders around this quiet neighborhood then take off running.

"You can't keep running away," Emily told me this afternoon while we sat on her deck and discussed everything from Cliff Booth to her Linus Project to my brief affair with Antonio.

"I'm not running. I'm doing my job and getting ready to find my own place."

Two miles from Emily's house the shower becomes a deluge. By the time I get back I'm drenched and chilled to the bone. Stripping off my wet clothes, I reach for a pair of jogging pants and a soft, fleecy sweatshirt, anything to make me feel cozy. Emily says it's nerves, and maybe she's half right. I read somewhere that if you're not acting your true self, your body rebels in ways you'd never imagine. For instance, I'm standing here wanting to wrap myself in a blanket, and in spite of the rain, the temperature is still hovering around the high sixties.

Maybe my true self is rebelling or maybe it's merely telling me I'm going crazy.

Reaching under the bed for my padded terry-cloth spa slippers, I encounter the box of letters. I take them out, sort them by date, then start opening and reading.

Dear Delta,
It's impossible to forget you. The beauty of what might have been haunts me.
  Don't throw us away because my mother scared you. Call me, beautiful lady. Until then, the phone will be my constant companion.
Yours,
Antonio

The phone rings, causing me to jump and scatter letters across the floor. When I say "Hello," and Buddy Earl says "Hello, yourself," I see my future—toddling into old age making excuses to suitors of his ilk or worse.

"I saw Emily leave with her new boyfriend," Buddy Earl says, "and I thought you might be lonely.

I could come over and we could watch some Saturday-night wrestling."

News travels fast in a town as small as Smithville, and usually it bears no resemblance to the truth.

"He's merely Emily's friend. I'm very busy right now. Listen, while I was out running I saw that nice woman who moved in down the street. Do you know her?"

"Yes, Doris Watson, schoolteacher over in Fulton, just got her divorce from Frank."

"Yes, that's the one. If I had time I'd go down and welcome her to the neighborhood, take some cookies or something."

Maybe he'll take the hint. On my hands and knees I pick up the spilled letters then walk to the window. Good Lord. This is what I have become: a lonely matchmaker who moons over love letters and keeps company with a cat.

I see Buddy Earl open his front door, carrying a small brown bag (cookies, I hope and not a tin of sardines). He slicks back his hair and then gets into his Ford pickup. He's not wearing his cowboy hat. This is progress.

How easy it is to fix the problems of others, and how hard to fix your own.

Sinking onto Emily's sofa, I open another letter.

Dear Delta,
Magic is rare and we found it. Please don't throw it away.
    Call me.
Yours,
Antonio

I don't know if Antonio really feels this way or if two weeks after I left he married a woman young enough to have many children and keep Gina's head out of the oven.

All of a sudden I feel as if I'm in the middle of the 1957 movie classic, *An Affair to Remember*. I can sit here on top of the Empire State Building wondering what happened or I can climb down and find out the truth.

I get off my Empire State Building and trudge down to the basement where I turn on my computer. But it's not work on my mind; it's finding some answers.

Emily

When we get back from the movies, Cliff takes my hand and says, "I'm having a good time, Emily."

"Me, too."

"I have to go back to Huntsville tomorrow, but I'll call you. Okay?"

"I'd like that very much."

He kisses my cheek then turns around and waves before he drives off. I look up at the stars and say thank you. There are all kinds of grace in the universe, and one is a man who understands how you can enjoy his company and still be wearing your late husband's ring.

I go down to the basement den where Delta is sitting at her computer.

"You're working late."

"I'm not working, I'm searching for my father."

I know better than to make a big to-do about Uncle Carl. I'm sure he's not the only father who left his family without a forwarding address. Besides, Delta hates being the center of her own soap opera, so all I say is, "Good."

My phone's ringing when I go upstairs.

"Hello, Emily. I made an ass of myself at the family reunion." Lucille never says hello and she never stays up past the ten o'clock news. This is serious.

"That's okay, Lucille. We all do sometimes."

"Are you dating that Booth fellow?"

"No. We're just friends, and if I ever decide I want more, I'll let everybody know so we can all deal with it."

There's a silence as big as Dallas from her end, then she starts crying. Old Stone Face. Of all things.

"Are you okay?" I ask.

"I just miss Mike, that's all."

"I do, too. Every single day. And not a day goes by that I don't love him. Please know that, Lucille. I loved your brother and that will never change. No matter what I decide to do about Cliff."

"Maybe I ought to tell you what Mike said."

"When?"

"Not long before he died." I stand very still while Lucille gets hold of herself. "He told me to tell you he didn't want you living by yourself, that you're too young and too full of life to spend the rest of your days mourning for him."

"Why didn't you tell me sooner?"

"I thought I'd never have to. And seeing Cliff Booth like that shocked my pants off. I don't want to think about you going off with somebody else and having a different life."

"Do you think I would forget about you, Lucille?"

"I reckon so. Who'd want a curmudgeonly old poop like me around?"

"I would. We've had our differences, but you're Mike's flesh and blood and I love you, even if you do sometimes drive me crazy."

"I drive everybody crazy. Don't plan on stopping, either. You can just put that in your pipe and smoke it, Emily Jones."

She's got her piss and vinegar back, and I'm glad. This is what family is all about, little hurts, disappointments and losses balanced by large doses of love, compassion and forgiveness.

We say goodbye before we get sentimental and start making greeting-card declarations. I'm hanging up when I hear Delta's footsteps on the basement stairs. She sinks onto the sofa and I sink into it with her. We both prop our feet on the coffee table.

"I'm going to miss this when you move out," I tell her.

"It'll be awhile yet. I found a lead for Carl Jordan. I'm heading to Florida tomorrow, and I don't know what in the world I'm going to say if I find him."

"You worry too much, Delta. Just say what's on your mind and in your heart."

"Currently my mind is a minefield and my heart is a wasteland."

"Good grief. Let's eat some pie."

I don't know why Delta has to make this a soap opera. I guess it's the writer in her.

Delta

Highway 95A in Molino, Florida, just north of Pensacola. Carl Jordan's last-known address. That makes sense to me. He loved two things, baseball and fishing. What he didn't love was being tied down to a family.

I turn onto the small, two-lane highway that

meanders through a neighborhood of nice houses. I can't picture him here. But when the road segues into a convenience store, several trailer houses and an abandoned school, I can see how he would end up here. It's only twenty miles from the bay in a place where you could know everybody along the road or nobody at all.

I turn around and backtrack to the convenience store. It's a modest-sized building in need of a good coat of paint and some serious parking-lot repair. According to his name tag the manager is James Deaton, a man graying at the temples but still so good to look at he ought to be a centerfold.

I adjust my sunglasses, smooth my travel-wrinkled slacks and approach the counter. I'll take the direct approach. *Do you know Carl Jordan?*

"Hello, Miss, can I help you?"

"Yes, do you…have any Diet Pepsi?"

"In the cooler along the back wall."

I escape then stand in front of the open glass door hoping the cool air will keep me from hyper-ventilating. I'm not the fainting, nervous type. I don't even flinch when I see an occasional snake in

Emily's backyard, as we did this morning before I set out on this six-hour fool's errand.

She screamed while I said, "Em, for Pete's sake, you're living by the water. What do you expect? Don't bother him and he won't bother you."

"I wasn't planning on inviting him to dinner."

I'm not going to invite Carl Jordan to dinner, either. I'm not even going to ask about him. I'm going to get into my Liberty Sport and go back to Smithville where I'll pack my bags and find a place of my own. Which is the only sensible thing to do.

"Miss?" The manager is looking at me as if I'm a victim of a hit and run. And maybe I am. Several hits and runs. "Are you all right?"

"Maybe I should sit down."

He leads me into his office, a charming space you wouldn't expect to find at the back of a store such as this one, neatly organized desk and file cabinets, rattan furniture with deep cushions, sprawling tropical plants in front of the windows.

"Let me get you some water."

While he leaves I take off my sweater. It's twenty

degrees hotter this far south, a factor I didn't consider when I set out in a wool blend twinset.

Me. A seasoned traveler. Forgetting the basic rule of traveling: pack for the climate.

"Thank you," I say when he hands me a tumbler of ice water.

James Deaton sits in the other rattan chair as relaxed and easygoing as if I'm his favorite cousin from Alabama and he's going to catch up on family news. This is one of the joys of traveling in the Deep South, the easy camaraderie of strangers.

"I thought you were going to pass out on me back there."

I feel guilty taking up his time. He has a store to run, customers to attend to.

"I'm sorry I frightened you. Really. I wanted to ask about Carl Jordan but I got scared and chickened out."

"Carl Jordan. Yeah, I know him. He used to come in here to pick up his fish bait."

"Do you know where he lives?"

"No, I haven't seen him in about two years."

Okay. I'll go home now. Maybe find an apartment

that allows dogs. Get a cute small breed. A sheltie or a Jack Russell terrier.

"But you might ask around at the video store on Highway 90 next to Winn Dixie. He was always talking about going in there renting movies."

I thank him once more, then climb back into my Jeep fully intending to head north. But the pull of feelings I don't recognize turns me south, and I drive until I find a Holiday Inn with beachfront access.

It's so hot down here I have to turn the air-conditioning on. I stow my suitcase full of unsuitable fall clothes, then head to Wal-Mart to rectify my mistake. In the crowded aisles, while I search for short-sleeved cotton blouses, my cell phone rings.

I say hello, half expecting Antonio's voice, but it's Emily. Why should a man who believed in the surprise of letters and singing love ballads underneath balconies bother to make a telephone call to a woman he hasn't seen in weeks?

"Did you find your father yet, Delta?"

"No. He's not here."

"Don't give up."

"I won't."

"That's didn't sound too convincing to me. Listen here, Delta, until you find Carl Jordan you're just going to keep on running, even from the really good men like Antonio."

Emily seems so sure that I'm looking for Carl Jordan to find some peace about men who love and leave. And maybe that's part of it, but the truth is, I'm searching for myself.

I don't want merely to survive. I want to triumph. To live with grace.

After we hang up I check out, then head back to the motel to work, but the Umbrian guide is too prickly tonight. Putting on my pink high-top jogging shoes and a good windbreaker against Pensacola Bay's evening breezes, I sprint down the beach with ghosts running alongside me.

Did I really fall for Antonio or was I merely seduced by the magic of the Green Heart of Italy?

Can I really find my father or am I chasing the dream of lost childhood?

When I was five we vacationed in Pensacola, if not on this very beach, then on one much like it.

"Don't go too far into the water," my mother cautioned, but Daddy said, "Let her play, Estelle, she's a strong swimmer."

Was that why he left, because he thought I was strong enough to swim in any current?

I drop to a sand dune and watch the moon.

Poets write lyrics about such a moon, ordinary people hold hands and cats stand on back fences and yowl. And all for what? Love? Or is it simply that seeing something so much bigger than yourself, so much more important and enduring, turns loose a river of emotion that has to be expressed?

I head back to the motel, but this time I'm not running away, I'm running toward.

Emily

It's raining and chilly. I grab my fuzzy blue robe and go into the bathroom to brush my teeth. Good grief. Delta was right. This robe is ready for a decent burial.

The idea makes me wince, and all of a sudden I see that I haven't been clinging to this robe because it's comfortable, but because Mike gave it to me. When? At least fifteen years ago.

I go into the kitchen and rummage around for garbage bags, take off my robe and drop it in then go back to my bedroom to find something cozy. One of Mike's sweaters. The gray cashmere. Turtleneck. Size extra large.

I'm just about to put it on and snuggle in when I hear Lucille chastising me about freezing old men. She's right, too. Winter will soon be here and there are people who will go cold because I'm hanging on to my husband's possessions. As if he'll say, *Wait, I can't go anywhere without my clothes*, then stroll back in and say, *Now that I'm back I might as well stay.*

I go down the hall to retrieve the bag, take it back to the bedroom and drop the gray sweater inside. What was so hard about that? I get dressed, pass by the bag on the way to make coffee, then backtrack and retrieve the sweater.

When my phone rings, Delta says, "Em. What are you doing?"

Standing here with my face buried in the sweater.

"I'm cleaning out Mike's closet. Sort of."

"Listen, I have a lead. Last night I decided to go to

the video store before it closed, and the woman there said she thought my father had moved to Demopolis."

"You passed right through there."

"I know. It's plausible he'd go there."

"Why?"

"Because of the Black Warrior River. I don't think he's going to get far from a body of water."

"Good luck."

"You, too, Em."

I'm going to need it. Each piece of clothing I put in this bag breaks my heart. But sometimes I think you have to go ahead and let your heart break a little in order to move forward.

Delta

I check out of the Holiday Inn and am back in Demopolis three hours after talking to Em. With all afternoon left to make inquiries, I don't find a motel but go immediately to the marina. If anybody knows about a man who loved water more than he loved his family, it will be the people at the docks.

"Yes, Carl Jordan was here."

The woman talking is Margie, who has an office filled with artificial poinsettias, a television going full blast with *Colombo* reruns and a sign out front advertising rental fishing boats.

"He stayed around about six months, more or less, then said he had to move on."

"Do you know where?"

"Said he had a friend with a cabin on a lake somewhere up north of here."

"Do you remember where?" I sound like the Gestapo. I smile to take the edge off.

"Mississippi, I think. Some little town that started with a C. Let's see, Colombo or something like that."

Why *wouldn't* she say that with the scruffy, trench-coated detective himself filling her TV screen?

"Could he have said Columbus?"

"Maybe."

That's not much to go on. And even if he has gone to Columbus, I don't have his friend's name. Really, I have nothing except a gut feeling that I'm on the right track.

When I climb back into my Liberty Sport and

turn the Jeep toward Columbus, it hits me that Carl Jordan has been migrating slowly north toward home.

He would be seventy now. In the end isn't that what all of us desire—to find a safe place, put our feet up and say, There now, I can rest, I'm home?

CHAPTER 16

Travel is a metaphor for life: the landscape constantly changes. Instead of clinging to the familiar, be open to the surprise and wonder of the unfamiliar.

The Seasoned Traveler's Guide to Umbria,
A work in progress, Delta Jordan

Emily

Delta and I are standing in an empty loft apartment in downtown Tupelo while the manager explains that the utilities are included in the rent. It's not electricity and water Delta's interested in, but the light pouring through a bank of high windows overlooking Main Street.

I know this. She hates being trapped by walls

and has always gravitated toward the light. Earth protects three sides of my basement but one faces the lake. Delta moved the desk so she could see through the French doors.

Maybe this is her way of always facing an escape route. Maybe this is why she was so disappointed when she came home yesterday and said she'd run into a dead end finding her father.

"The only public lake I could find in Columbus was Officer's Lake," she told me. "Nobody there had ever heard of him."

"There must be dozens of private lakes."

"Finding them would take weeks, maybe even years."

"You could hire a private detective."

"No, Em. In all these years he's never tried to find me. Carl Jordan doesn't want to be found. End of story."

Now she's saying to the apartment's manager, "I'll take it."

While she's signing the lease I walk to the windows to check out the view. Across the street is the Gum Tree Museum of Art. My Lord, that's where Antonio's paintings will hang.

I hear the manager leave, hear Delta come up behind me. "You saw this?"

"Yes. It had nothing to do with renting this apartment. Everything I need is within walking distance—great downtown restaurants, the library, the post office. If I want to be entertained I can just walk downstairs and sit at the Main Attraction's coffee bar and watch the customers discovering funky treasures. Antonio had nothing to do with this."

That's not so, is what I'm thinking, but I'm not one of those righteous, know-it-all friends so all I say is, "Let's get you moved in."

Delta

The advantage of not being weighed down by personal possessions is that moving and settling in takes two days instead of two weeks.

My desk is by the windows facing the gallery, and I'm sitting here now watching covered canvases being carried inside. Antonio's show. I glance at my calendar and mark an X across the date. Only two more days till his gala opening.

I wonder if the painting I love best will be in the show. Antonio poured all the light of the universe onto that canvas and when you stand underneath, it spills over you. Like sunshine. Like a blessing. Like hope.

My phone rings, and I jump as if I've been caught spying.

"You left your pink running shoes here," Em says. "If you need them, I'll drive over."

"Not unless you're coming this way. I don't need them." Not today, at least.

"Okay, great. I'm taking Leo to the vet for his annual checkup, then I'm meeting Glenda Noles about converting a rental warehouse on my downtown Smithville property to a place for the local Linus Project."

"I'm glad to see you doing something you love, Em."

"Yeah. Me, too. So what's happening over your way? Anything exciting?"

"No."

Then I tell her about the arrival of Antonio's paintings so she won't get the big idea that I'm still harboring any hope in that direction. After we hang up I start assembling my notes, but my doorbell rings. What next?

There's a courier in my hallway with a very large package. Since nobody but Em knows I live here, I tell him, "I'm Delta Jordan. You must have the wrong address."

"No, ma'am. This is for you. Sign here, please."

There's no mistaking the size and shape of the package. I'm almost afraid to open it, knowing its contents could rip open an old wound and leave me bleeding on the floor.

Or else wishing I hadn't left my running shoes at Em's.

The paper crackles as I peel it away. Bit by bit the light from this magnificent canvas pours into my loft, across my heart, over my spirit. It's Antonio's *Speranza*. Hope.

And attached to the back is a letter.

Dear Delta,
I think you Americans call this a housewarm-

ing gift. I hope you can find a place for it in your new apartment. When you look at it, think of me as I think of you. Daily. And always with a smile.

Yours,

Antonio

Standing in the path of oil-on-canvas light, I hold the letter over my heart and just stand there, trying to take it all in. The letter is typical of Antonio—written with moving simplicity and grace, telling me nothing, telling me everything.

Whether I ever see its creator again, the painting is mine. If I send it back I've insulted him, and I would never do that. I finally rouse myself from this spell and walk through my apartment, trying to decide where it should go.

It's perfect over the bed, but hanging it there is too heart-wrenching. Besides, this painting should be the first thing you see when you come into my apartment. After forty-eight years of holing up in functional spaces that don't carry a single hint of a home, a whit of personality, a drop of welcome, I'm ready for a place that says, "Come in, sit down, breathe, laugh, sing and most of all, let yourself hope."

These ceilings are twelve feet tall. I'll need a ladder and Luther, the custodian, to hang the painting. I lean it carefully against the wall, stand back to admire it from all angles then call Luther.

After we get it on the wall, I call Em.

"You knew Antonio was sending the painting."

"No, all I knew was that he asked Cliff for your address. I'm coming right over to see it."

"Bring my running shoes."

"Oh, Delta."

"Just bring them, that's all."

After we hang up I sit on the floor in front of my painting and feel as if I'm free falling from a hot-air balloon.

There's another letter waiting for me the next morning.

Dear Delta,

At last I am in your city. I'll pick you up at your apartment this evening. We'll have dinner and talk. I will hold your hand and kiss you, and if you will allow me, I'll show you feelings that are real and true and capable of overcoming every one of your misgivings.

Unless you call and tell me no, I'll be there at seven.

Yours,

Antonio

I won't let myself think about this evening. Tucking the letter into my jeans pocket, I go to my desk and put another X on my calendar. One day before he becomes the toast of the town. Women will cast themselves at his feet. Young women with wrinkle-free skin and flat bellies. Fetching, nubile females with trim waists and fertile eggs.

I call Em and say I can't possibly go. She tells me I can't possibly turn him down.

"You deserve something good, Delta. If you don't go, I'll be mad at you forever."

"Next week's your birthday."

"Well, I won't start getting mad until after I get my present. I miss having you here, Delta."

"I miss you, too, but I don't miss the cat."

"I've been thinking about something a lot, lately."

"What?"

"If you want to know the truth, sex. Or the lack thereof. And what's appropriate and what's not."

"Just go with your heart, Em."

"That's great advice. Why don't you ever take it? I know darned good and well you left your heart in Italy, and now it's coming back to you, and if you don't grab it and hang on, I'm coming over there to whip your butt."

"Good grief. Do you have an orchestra with violins over there? The next thing I know you'll be singing 'I Left My Heart in San Francisco.'"

"Seriously, Delta. You'll see him tomorrow night at the opening, anyway. I know you wouldn't miss that."

"No. I wouldn't."

"Okay, then. What's one night early?"

One night early is being alone with him. One night early is having him here in the privacy of my apartment. One night early is paradise. Or hell. Whichever way you want to look at it.

What am I supposed to do now? Here I am for the first time in years harboring feelings that are real, and that scares me to death. Am I supposed to sit down and say, "Listen, Antonio, I'm not going to see you unless you give me a contract signed in blood that you'll never walk out the door and leave me to wonder what I did wrong?"

Instead, I work through the day with one eye on the clock, then take a bath at six, put on black slacks and a green blouse at six-thirty and sit on the edge of my seat until seven.

Of course, he might not come. That's what I'm thinking when the doorbell rings. He's standing in my hallway looking so wonderful he has to be out of my reach, while I hang onto the doorknob and try to get my tongue unglued from the roof of my dry mouth.

"Hello, beautiful lady."

He sweeps through the door, closes it behind him and solves my most immediate problem. There's no need for speech when somebody is kissing you as if he's just returned from war. There's no need for uncertainty when somebody lifts you off your feet, whisks you to the bedroom and undresses you as if you're such a magnificent gift he doesn't want to mar the wrapping. There's no need for food when the only taste you desire is the hard angle between his neck and shoulder and the sweat-salty skin of his inner thigh.

Afterward neither of us thinks about food for a long time. We lie together with our hands linked and our thighs touching while I tell him about the three men who walked out and my search for my father, and he tells me about the serious talk he had with his mother.

"Her dreams are not mine, Delta. She knows this now. It feels as if I've waited several lifetimes for you. For this." He kisses the tips of my fingers, one by one. "You should know I don't dissuade easily. You should also know that I'm planning to stay in America for a while, to paint. And to woo you."

"I'm wooed. I'm wowed." I'm also giggling like a schoolgirl. "And I'm hungry."

We go into my kitchen and heat a can of chicken noodle soup, which is the standard remedy for sick people. And maybe I've been sick for a very long time. Maybe now I'm getting better. If I can have a steady dose of soup and Antonio, perhaps I'll even get well.

* * *

When you're over forty, the good thing about morning is knowing you have another day to charge forward. The bad thing is that everything looks different in the cold light of day. Sometimes better, but more often than not, worse.

Take my face, for instance. While Antonio's in the kitchen making coffee I'm staring at the sheet creases in my left cheek and wanting to slap the mirror. No wonder Gina wanted to send me back and get a younger model for her gorgeous son. No wonder I haven't had a call for dates by anybody except Howdy Doody in the last six years.

Antonio comes up behind me, puts his arms around me and kisses my cheek. The wrinkled one. As if he didn't notice.

Maybe he needs glasses. Maybe I need a mental examination.

"I have to go to the gallery and take care of a few details."

"Okay." I turn sideways, putting my good side toward him. Would it always be like this? An older woman trying to make sure a younger man doesn't see her in unflattering poses? "I'll see you tonight."

That sounds easy enough. But after the door shuts behind him it feels as if I've committed myself to climbing Mount Everest. I put on sweats and scramble around in my closet till I find my running shoes then take off down Main Street. I'm hoping to catch all the green lights, hoping I can cross the railroad track before one of the trains that blocks traffic in every direction hurls into downtown Tupelo and stops my pell-mell rush.

I beat the morning train, pound past City Hall, get caught by a red light crossing Elizabeth Street, then finally end up on the walking track, my lungs burning and my spirits alternately sagging and soaring.

Why? That's what I want to know. Why did they all leave?

My cell phone rings, and I'm grateful for an excuse to sit down.

"Delta, I've got these glow-in-the-dark condoms, and I'm fixing to use them."

Lord, Em always does everything as if a circus has come to town and she's in the center ring.

"When?"

"I don't know. As soon as I get up the courage."

"You called so I'd encourage you or discourage you?"

"I'm not sure."

"Listen, Em, maybe you ought to wait until you're absolutely positive this is what you want."

"I feel like I'm fixing to explode. You know how I sleep like a rock? Well, last night I didn't sleep a wink."

"Take some Tylenol PM."

"It's not the same thing."

"I know, but it'll make you sleep."

She sighs, then says, "Listen to me going on about myself. I called to see how it went last night."

"We're both the same. Antonio's incredible and I'm confused."

"Oh, Lord, Delta, who's not?"

That may be the wisest thing I've ever heard Em say. Life is never going to be easy. Sure, there's joy, but there will always be moments of grief and confusion and rage. And who knows? Maybe it takes those bad moments to make us appreciate the good.

"Delta, are you still there?"

"I'm here, Em."

I *am* here. And if I can't take complete charge of the direction I'm going, at least I can do my best to make sure I don't get knocked too far off course.

I leave the park and head back to my apartment, this time sprinting because I'm eager to get home. Dragging out my step stool, I take a shoe box from the top closet shelf and spread the photographs across my bed—my past captured in three-by-five, black-and-white glossies.

Somewhere in here is bound to be a clue to my father's whereabouts.

There are pictures of me on six birthdays, blowing out candles, my beautiful mother standing behind my chair and smiling into the camera. After that, there are no more birthday photographs, no more cakes and happy smiles and candles to mark the passing of time.

There's a picture of me with Mac, the border collie I begged for and got on my ninth birthday, both of us gazing into the distance as if we're searching for something. There's a studio photograph of my mother, probably in her late teens, probably before she met my daddy, because she's smiling and looking as if she believes in a future full of wonderful surprise.

But where's Carl Jordan? I dig through my school pictures and finally find one—Daddy with a friend I don't know. I'm torn between ripping it to shreds and flushing it down the toilet—psychic separation—and crying.

In the end, I do neither. I put it in my pocket, pat it and say, "There." I don't know why. If I could answer the question why, I guess I'd be the smartest person in the universe.

CHAPTER 17

The winding streets of Spoleto remind me
of life. If you wear sturdy shoes and plant your
feet solidly, the cobblestones won't trip you.
    The Seasoned Traveler's Guide to Umbria,
            A work in progress, Delta Jordan

Emily

Cliff drove over, and we're in the Gum Tree
Museum of Art listening to the mayor present
Antonio a key to the city.

"It's rare for our town to have an artist of such
stature. Thanks to the efforts of our fine director,
we're happy to welcome Antonio Donacelli from
Piediliuco, Italy."

Everybody's applauding, including me, but I'm standing here thinking the mayor should have acknowledged Delta. And even Cliff. They're the reasons Antonio came to Tupelo.

Cliff nudges me and I realize I'm still clapping after everybody else has stopped. Which just goes to show my mind is not on art.

"Em?" It's Delta, wearing green, but not the color of my condoms. *Oh, help*. And it's perfectly clear from the way she glows what she's been up to. "May I have a private moment with you?"

We weave our way through this capacity crowd, the biggest our gallery has ever seen, I'd say. When we get to the ladies' room, Delta says she's been going through her mother's old photographs.

"I found this." She takes a snapshot out of her purse of two men leaning against the porch railing of the fifties-style house where they lived when we were children. "Do you know who that is with Daddy?"

Uncle Carl is the handsome one. I used to pretend he was a movie star and that Delta and I were pampered Hollywood princesses. The other man is short and square with a nose that seems too big for his face.

"I don't."

"Think, Em. It's the only clue I have about who my daddy might have contacted after he left Demopolis."

I was nine when Uncle Carl left, old enough to remember, and it's important to Delta that I do. Closing my eyes I see Uncle Carl with his fishing pole. But I see Mike, too, and that confuses the issue.

Uncle Carl fished mostly at Pickwick. He always wore a straw fedora that looked like something Bugsy Segal might have worn, and sometimes he'd bring fresh tomatoes to our house on his way to the lake.

Vernon Waycaster brought these, he'd say.

"That's it," I tell Delta. "Vernon Waycaster. He had a farm somewhere south of here, and he used to bring fresh vegetables every time he went fishing with Uncle Carl."

"Could it have been Columbus? Do you remember?"

"I don't, but yes, it could have been."

Delta hugs me. "Thanks, Em."

"So, what's next?"

"I'm hiring a private detective. Now that I have a name, I might have a shot at success."

I reach for her hands, which are far too cold for late fall in a perfectly heated building. Stress always turns her extremities into ice blocks. When she'd sleep over at my house, right after Uncle Carl left, I'd make her get up and put on socks. I think she still sleeps in them from early fall to late spring. And sometimes in summer when the air-conditioning is turned too high.

"Let's get back inside," Delta says.

I follow her back to the gallery where Cliff and Antonio are making plans for a late-night dinner, a foursome, which is fine with me. With the goods in my purse, I feel like a criminal planning a major crime wave. I keep expecting somebody to tap me on the shoulder and say, "I'm on to you. Hand over those condoms."

I wonder if I should call the children first. I wonder if I should call Lucille. "Listen, I just wanted to let you know I'm planning to have sex, if that's all right with you."

When Cliff touches my elbow I jump as if Lucille has caught me with my hand on his zipper.

"Is Woody's all right with you?"

"Sure. Anywhere's fine."

Woody's Restaurant has fine table linen, long tablecloths that hide what a wandering hand might do. Good heavens. I excuse myself, leave the three of them talking to Antonio's admiring fans, then go into the ladies' room again and look at my flushed face in the mirror. My flushed, scared face. Apparently my body wants something that the rest of me does not.

"I'm sorry, Mike," I whisper, and he says, *It's okay, Em. It's time to move on.*

I sit on the toilet and study my swollen feet. I'm not used to wearing shoes with three-inch heels. In spite of thinking—hoping—I have Mike's permission, I wonder if this is a punishment.

Widow's feet swell twice the size of Texas for thinking about intimacy less than a year after her husband's death.

Is there a timetable for this sort of thing? Lucille would know. I wonder where she gets her information. Emily Post?

I hold out my left hand, turn the ring round and round my finger, feel the heat coming from that eternal circle of gold. "I love you, Mike," I say. "I'll always love you." And then I slide my wedding ring off and slip it into my purse.

"Em?" Delta's back, worried.

"I'm okay." I stand up, don't faint.

"You're sure?"

"Really."

It's true. Actually I'm a bit giddy, almost like the sixteen-year-old girl who cheered from the sidelines while Cliff pitched a perfect, shutout game.

"Okay, great. The men are ready to eat."

So am I. But not with a fork.

Dinner is fine. No hands under the table. No sly glances. Just four people laughing and talking about art and travel (Delta and Antonio) and baseball and the Linus Project (Cliff and me).

It's the after-dinner part that I don't know how to cope with. From the look on Delta's face when she drove off with Antonio I'd say she's doing fine with this part. I'd even say she's learning to excel.

When Cliff takes me home, I stand at my front

door like a barber pole. Good grief. What made me think I'd look good in a red-and-white striped blouse, the stripes going around?

"I guess I'd better be going," Cliff says, and I jerk out of my barber-pole mode and say, "No. Don't."

Now I sound like a desperate housewife. Maybe I ought to be on TV.

"Won't you come in for coffee and dessert?"

"I'd like that very much."

In my kitchen I relax into my hostess mode, the woman who knows her way around a coffeepot better than anyone in northeast Mississippi. Shoot, maybe in the whole state.

I rummage in the icebox, take out a lemon pie and thaw it briefly in the microwave before I cut two slices. This is the last of Laura's pies, the last time I'll have to look at one and remember her standing in my doorway saying, *I hope he can eat this. It's so sad to think of Mike Jones as one of our sick and afflicted.*

Suddenly I lose my appetite for late-night pie in the kitchen and midnight sex in my bedroom. The room where my husband used to wrap me in his arms and legs, even after he was so sick that's all he could do.

"I love you, baby," I'd whisper, and he'd kiss the top of my head, hold me so close I believed he'd never leave, believed we'd go to the hospital the next day and the doctors would say, "We made a mistake. Sorry about all that chemo."

"Emily?" Cliff comes up behind me, puts his hand on my shoulders. "What's wrong?"

"I was thinking about Mike."

He puts his arms around me, rocks me as if I'm six years old, then kisses my cheek.

"Let's have coffee another time."

"Yes. Another time."

"You want to go to the movies tomorrow night?"

"Yes."

A crowded theater, lots of popcorn with butter, somebody funny on the screen, perhaps Johnny Depp. Funny as well as good to look at.

"I'd like that," I add.

After Cliff leaves I go into my bedroom, take my wedding ring out of my purse and put it on my bedside table. Once I knew a widow who added rubies and emeralds and had hers made into a brooch that looked like a Christmas tree.

I'll be more tasteful than that. Maybe I'll add some topaz and make something hopeful, something that looks like a sunflower.

Delta

"I couldn't do it," Em says.

She and I are having lunch at Finney's Sandwich Shop while she tells me about her failed attempt at ending the celibacy of widowhood.

"All of me was willing except my heart."

"That's the most important thing."

Of course, I'm thinking of myself, remembering how Antonio put my hand over his heart and said, "It beats for you, Delta."

He is a complete romantic, one of those men you read about in the best love stories and wish you could have but know you probably won't. Ever. The universe produces about one in seven million, I think.

I don't know how I ever got lucky enough to find one. I don't even know if it will last. That's one of the reasons Em and I are headed to the offices of Boomer and Brown, Investigative Services. I'm going to do everything I can to ensure that this time, the man stays.

We finish our coconut pie, then climb into my Liberty Sport and drive to the address on Gloster Street, a brick house painted gray that was once a private residence.

"Boomer, here."

A man the size of the Grand Tetons crushes my hand, then escorts Em and me into an office so cluttered it looks as if he's packing for the movers.

"Make yourself at home." He sweeps magazines off a chair, sits down and props his feet on a Christmas popcorn tin. "Move some of that junk out of the way and sit down."

I'll bet this man can't even find his fountain pen. How in the world will he ever find Carl Jordan?

I hand him the photograph, identify Daddy and Vernon Waycaster then bring him up-to-date on my search.

"Do you think you can find him?"

"I'm known as Bird-Dog Boomer. If I can't, nobody can. But it could take a while and I'm not cheap."

I picture myself watching my life's savings flow into the coffers of Bird-Dog Boomer while I'm losing my hair, my teeth and my sex appeal.

Em nudges me. "Go for it, Delta. The prize is worth the pain."

"Okay. Done."

The deposit check I write Boomer would probably buy Little Rock, Arkansas. As we leave the offices Em says, "Think of it as an investment in your future."

In my pell-mell rush to find Daddy, I was thinking about my past, not my future. I was thinking I'd find out why he left.

Now I'm wondering what I'll do if Boomer finds him and he stays.

I say as much to Emily when we leave the office.

"Delta, do you know what your problem is?"

"No, but I guess you're going to tell me."

"You worry about stuff that hasn't even happened yet. Just quit it."

"It's not that simple."

"Yes, it is. Worry about something more important."

"Like what?"

"Sex."

"Oh, Lord, here we go again."

"Yeah, well, Cliff invited me to spend the weekend at his cabin on Smith Lake and I said yes."

"And now you're wishing you'd said no?"

"No, I'm wishing I had a crystal ball so I could see how all this is going to turn out."

"Well, you don't and neither do I."

"My point exactly. Go ahead and live, Delta. Nobody has a crystal ball."

Sometimes I think Em is getting too big for her britches.

CHAPTER 18

The Makahiki Festival, a reenactment of the ancient celebration of peacetime, was designed to give the people of Oahu a break from war. Perhaps we should initiate such festivities for ourselves, set aside times to say, Okay, today I'm not going to fret and fight, I'm going to step back and appreciate the joys of living.

The Seasoned Traveler's Guide to Hawaii,
Delta Jordan

Emily

Yesterday I was only half kidding Delta about the crystal ball. When Cliff called to invite me here the first thing he asked was, "Have you ever been to Smith Lake?"

"No."

"Good. We'll take things slow and easy. No expectations. You can lie around in the hammock with a good book while I fish and putter around the grill. There are two bedrooms and two baths, so you don't have to worry about a thing."

"Can I bring my cat?"

He said yes, and now here I am standing in his amazing cabin with sun pouring through skylights and a separate guest wing, and I'm not worrying about Leo at all; I'm worrying about which direction to go. And not just for this weekend, but afterward, too.

If I do give in to my insistent hormones and enjoy an intimate relationship with Cliff this weekend, does that mean I've made some kind of commitment? Does that mean he'll expect invitations to all my holiday parties and I'll expect my family to look at him sitting at my table and not resent that he's the wrong man, that he's not Mike?

"Em? Is anything wrong?"

"Life is so complicated."

"Not this weekend. Life is as simple as climbing

into that hammock on the porch and reading *Wuthering Heights* again."

"How did you know?"

"I have my ways." He walks to the wall of bookshelves beside a stone fireplace, pulls the book out and hands it to me.

"Now, scoot."

"What are you going to do?"

"Unload the bags then grab a fishing pole and catch the granddaddy of all catfish. I'm hankering for fried fish and hush puppies for supper."

"Mine are the best in two counties."

"Who said you were going to cook, Miss Priss? I'm the chef this weekend."

"Then what am I?"

"The pampered princess."

Mike made me his pampered princess and I played that role for thirty years. Now that I'm gaining a bit of self-sufficiency I'm not about to slide backward.

"I don't want to be a princess."

"My wives said I was an arrogant jackass who only knew about making money, and I want to prove them wrong."

"What do you want me to do? Call them up and say, Hey you made a big mistake?"

"Who lit a fire under your tail?"

Forget invitations to Thanksgiving and Christmas and worrying what the family will say. The way things are going I'll be lucky to survive the weekend.

"I'm just not fixing to fall back into that helpless trap, that's all."

"I don't want to trap you, Em. Just pet you. What's wrong with that?"

"Actually, I like to be petted."

"First you say you don't, then you do. I'll never understand women."

He grabs his fishing pole and stalks off.

"I didn't handle that well at all." I say this out loud but nobody hears me except a cardinal on the front-porch railing.

If Delta were here I'd discuss this with her, but she's not and I'm not fixing to pick up the phone and bother her. Again. As usual.

If I really want to be something other than a pampered princess, then I'd better stop acting like one.

But first I want to climb in that lovely hammock, cover myself against fall's chill with the soft throw from Cliff's couch, dive between the covers of this wonderful book and spend an hour or two in blessed forgetfulness.

Delta

The first thing I see when I wake up is Antonio on the other side of my bed. He sleeps with a half smile on his face and the deep, boneless contentment of a man who knows where he's going and what he wants. I finger-brush his hair away from his face, knowing this won't wake him, loving this private moment when I can lean on my elbow and drink in the sight of him.

For a long while I watch the sunlight track across his face then I ease out of bed and into the kitchen to make coffee. There's a note on the table, written on the thick Italian paper I know so well.

My dearest Delta,
You are my sun, my moon, my universe. I

love you today and shall love you all the days
of my life.

Yours,

Antonio

I picture him climbing out of bed in the middle
of the night, making his way through my apartment
in the dark and sitting at the table to put on paper
the exact words I need to hear. Affirmations of love.
Almost a guarantee, really, that he won't be like all
the others and walk out on a whim.

Not only does Antonio have an appreciation of
the human form in all its guises, but he also has an
instinctive understanding of the varied, glorious
and messy needs of two-legged mortals.

And I would be a complete fool to let that go.

"Good morning, beautiful lady." He glances at
the clock, laughs. "Or is it afternoon?"

I look up and think I must be the luckiest woman
in the universe. How many other women have the
world's most beautiful man standing naked in their
kitchen doorway?

"Thank you for the note."

He leans down, cups my face between his hands, looks deep into my eyes.

"Every day of my life I will write of my love for you. And someday you will believe me."

I want to be this woman, be loved by this man, forever.

I wonder how many women have this. I wonder how many women are sitting at their kitchen tables thinking about taking out the garbage instead of remembering the touch of a hand on a cheek, the feel of lips on top of the head, the assurance of a solid wall of chest blocking out everything except kindness and love.

And aren't they the same thing?

"Do you want croissants and cheese?" I ask, and when he says yes, we move toward the bank of windows and eat in the sunlight.

"I want to travel to your Mississippi Delta. I want to see and to paint an entire region that bears your name."

"Today?"

"Yes. And you will go with me. No excuses accepted."

"How did you know?"

"I read every thought in your lovely face."

In any other man I would perceive his command as arrogance, but in Antonio I see only the old-world courtliness of an ardent suitor who wants to be with his chosen woman.

I think about staying here in case Em needs me or Bird-Dog Boomer finds Daddy. Then I realize I'd merely be making excuses because there's a lost little girl inside me who is still afraid the cutest puppy in the pet shop window is not for her.

"Have computer, will travel."

He bends over and kisses my hand, then heads toward the bathroom. Soon I hear the rich cadences of his voice singing love songs in Italian. And I don't want to be anywhere but close enough to know he's singing for me.

Emily

I'm snoring so loud I wake myself up and nearly fall out of the hammock. This is no way for a self-avowed reformed princess to act. I heave myself out, fold the chenille throw and take it inside along with the book, then march down to the lake's edge where Cliff is casting for catfish. Or bass. I forget which.

"Do you have a pole?"

"Sometimes."

He never cracks a smile, just makes a perfect cast into a shady spot near a fallen log and keeps on fishing.

"Smart aleck." I spot another fishing pole on the bank, rummage in his gear box for the right lure, then make a perfect cast.

"Been keeping secrets, have you?"

"Plenty. I'm a self-sufficient woman of mystery, intrigue and romance, if I decide not to have a headache."

"I'll try not to give you one."

"Good. See that you don't."

We hush talking so we won't scare away our prey, then fish side by side till the sun goes down. If this were the movies I'd catch a record-sized fish on my first throw and then five more in quick succession, which would strike wonder and amazement in Cliff's heart. But it's real life and all I catch is an old rubber tire. Furthermore, I'm not after wonder and amazement. Just a little admiration and a lot of respect.

"How are you with peanut butter and crackers for supper?" he asks, and I say fine.

We head toward the house and I spread the peanut butter while he finds logs for the fire. Then we sit on sofa cushions he tosses onto the floor and eat everything on the plate. He gets the jar of peanut butter and two spoons and we eat till we have to unbutton our waistbands.

Cliff gives me this *look*, and I give it right back, and all of a sudden we're unbuttoning our shirts and everything else that stands in the way. The fire sends shadows over our skin and I am a woman with nothing on my mind except the relief he can give me with his talented lips and hands. By the time he gets around to my more interesting body parts I'm almost too excited to remember my name.

But I do. I also remember the story of a woman who thought she had a tumor when she was my age, but it turned out to be twins who made her live down the question, "Are these your grandchildren?"

"Wait."

I scurry to my purse to retrieve the slim package while Cliff turns off the lights, and for a while we laugh at how he looks green and glowing in the dark. Then we don't laugh anymore because we're busy washing away months of loneliness.

I don't think about Mike at all until I wake up tangled in Cliff's legs and the chenille throw he pulled off the sofa to cover us. There's a faint glow of dawn against the windowpanes, and I tiptoe so I won't wake Cliff.

In the semidarkness Mike is as real to me as if he's walking beside me on the way to the bathroom. There's a tender benevolence in his face that says *It's okay, Em. I understand.*

I sit in the dark on the toilet seat and say to him, "Cliff and I didn't use the *L*-word." My husband smiles at me then fades into the wallpaper.

I thought I would be different after last night. I thought I'd feel romantic and alluring, a woman on the brink of being part of a couple. But I don't. Instead I'm a woman who still loves her deceased husband, but who took care of her needs with a man for whom she has a tender regard.

I guess that makes me modern. Actually, I don't care what label you put on it. It feels great not to wake up wanting to claw the walls and chew the newspaper to bits.

It's cold in this dark bathroom, and when I get up to wrap myself in a towel I see the faint glow of green. Good grief. It's me, glowing in the dark.

The old me would turn this into a funny story at parties, but the new me hurries out of the bathroom to find the condom wrapper. "For decorative use only."

I wonder if I'll spend the rest of my life green and glowing. How will I ever explain that to my gynecologist?

Delta

I wake up slowly, the sound of last night's Delta blues and Antonio's Italian endearments still echoing in my mind.

Reaching toward his side of the bed, I find nothing but empty space. Suddenly chilled, I wrap the blanket around me, afraid even to call his name. What if there's no answer? What if he's gone?

There's a clock ticking somewhere in this hotel room that sounds like a time bomb, a faucet dripping water that might as well be Niagara Falls, a tomcat yowling on a fence in a lovesick voice that carries all the way to the Mississippi River.

I want to join him on the fence, to yowl and complain and rage against the fates and the bad decisions that brought me to this bed. Alone. Instead I sneak out of my covers and grab my robe. In the bathroom I find a fat envelope I'm scared to open.

Finally, though, I do.

Dearest Delta,
You were so beautiful sleeping I didn't want to wake you. I'm beside the river, painting. Join me when you can and I will wrap you in my arms and kiss you until you believe that I will love you forever.
Yours,
Antonio

I brush my teeth, rake a comb through my hair, grab my clothes and race toward the door. The wind ruffles my hair and the concrete chills my feet. Laughing, I hurry back inside for my shoes.

As I cut toward the path that leads to the river and Antonio, I vow that today I will think of nothing except possibilities.

CHAPTER 19

Sometimes a place you revisit has changed beyond recognition and even memories. This is as true of emotional places as it is the bricks and mortar of our childhood.

> *The Seasoned Traveler's Guide to*
> *Southern Restaurants,*
> Delta Jordan

Emily

I'm back home from Smith Lake after six laughter-filled days and Cliff's back in Huntsville.

If anybody asks me whether I'm falling in love with him, I'd have to say no. If they ask me whether I had a big itch that he scratched, I'd say absolutely.

If they said, Are you still glowing green? I'd say Thank God, no.

I don't know when I changed from this big romantic who drools over Heathcliff and Rhett Butler to somebody who discreetly and discriminately takes care of her needs, but somewhere along the way I did.

And I'm not a bit sorry. Maybe the laughter and easy companionship and good sex will turn into love and maybe not. All I know is that I've lost the desire to report anything to Lucille and my children. I'm having a relationship. Period. Let them deal with it.

When my doorbell rings, I say hello to Glenda Noles then offer her pear pie and coffee while we talk about the stock options and the Linus Project. She eats two pieces and I'm copying the recipe for her when Delta's number pops up on my cell phone.

I could call her back, but the prickling at the back of my neck says this is important. I excuse myself then walk onto the deck to answer.

"Em, Bird-Dog Boomer has found Daddy."

I have to sit down. "Oh, Lord, Delta. Where?"

"He's at his friend's private lake in Columbus. Just as I suspected."

"That's wonderful."

I hope. *Please, God, let it be wonderful for her.*

"Where are you now?" I ask.

"We're still in Clarksdale. Antonio's working on the most incredible painting and I've decided to write a guide to Mississippi blues."

"My Lord, Delta, do you ever think about resting? Nobody can work all the time."

"Em, the music here is amazing. I've found out there are some great blues musicians in the hill country, too. And the music there is a bit different from Delta blues."

This sharp left turn in conversation is the audible equivalent of Delta putting on her running shoes.

"Delta, when are you seeing Uncle Carl?"

"Tomorrow… I hate to leave… Still…"

"Keep your chin up. Change is hard. What can I do to help?"

"Just say a prayer."

"I will."

This time, though, my prayer is to Mike. *Darling, I don't know how much you can do now, but if you can work miracles, now's the time.*

I go back inside, pour two cups of fresh coffee then lay plans with Glenda to send out the first batch of blankets to the small, needy angels of this world.

Delta

Antonio wanted to come with me, to be there to hold my hand when I first meet Daddy, but I told him no, thank you. This is something I have to do by myself no matter how scared and tongue-tied I am.

Besides, I want to think of him painting beside the river and standing in the shower singing Italian love songs and sprawled on the bed waiting for me. I don't know what I'm going toward, but I want to believe I have something to go back to.

Although it's only eleven o'clock I stop for lunch at a roadside barbecue place so at least I'll be well fed for this confrontation. I don't even know what to call him. *Daddy* is what I used to say, but after all these years of absence I don't think he deserves that title.

"Hot or mild?"

I start to say I haven't noticed the weather, when I come to myself. The waitress is standing beside my table with her feet swollen over her shoes and a pencil poised over her order pad, and she's asking about barbecue sauce, not this warm Indian summer day we often get in October in the Deep South.

"Mild," I tell her.

After she leaves I take a packet of letters from my purse and spread them across the table where they lie, rich and important-looking, my day-to-day promises from Antonio as a man willing to go the distance.

Really, these letters are about as close to a guarantee as I'm going to get. The one I open was on my pillow this morning

My beloved Delta,
Although you don't complain, I can see in your lovely face you're scared about meeting the man who is your father. Be yourself with him no matter what he is like, what he says or what he has done. Take the high road and know that I am with you, holding your hand.
Forever yours,
Antonio

I trace Antonio's words with my fingertips, make a mantra of *take the high road*, then fold the letter and slip it back into its envelope. The waitress is coming my way with food, so I slide the letters back into my purse, grateful today for three things: Antonio's letters, Daddy's willingness to see me and good barbecue.

Then I climb into my Liberty Sport and head toward a rendezvous with my past.

Emily

Delta left today and Cliff called before lunch to tell me he'd be back in Tupelo next week and I'm thinking sexy new nighties and sweaty thighs while I stand in my bare feet talking to Lucille about Thanksgiving turkey.

"I thought I'd have hot dogs this year," I tell her. "Not make a big deal of it. Just curl up with a paper plate and watch the Macy's Thanksgiving Day parade."

"I know how you feel. Without Mike nothing's the same. Why don't you and the kids drive down to Texas and let me put on a spread at the ranch?"

Oh, Lord. Boots and bowlegged swagger and braying talk about the past.

I glance out my window to see Buddy Earl going into his house with the divorcée from down the street. The way they're all hugged up, it looks as if romance is blooming under my nose.

I wonder what they'll do for Thanksgiving. I wonder about Glenda Noles, who, because of her size and her penchant for going from port to port without real connections, seems to be the *Titanic* adrift in the Atlantic, and Cliff, who was merely adrift till he met me. Or so he says.

Then there's Delta. And Antonio, if he's not in Italy, and even Rosa.

What I want to do is move on toward the future. Create some new traditions. Or no traditions at all. Just be spontaneous, do whatever suits me at the moment.

"Listen, Lucille. I want you and the children to come here, as usual."

"Great. I think Mike would like it that you're keeping tradition alive."

Mike would be the last person to root for tradition in the face of an overhauled life. Sure, he kept up the facade the last three years he lived, but only because he wanted his family around him, wanted us to be hopeful.

I tell Lucille I have to go because of call waiting. It's Delta.

"Have you seen him yet?" I ask.

"No. I'm sitting on the side of the road within walking distance of the driveway, but I can't make myself go in. I can't make myself walk up to a man I don't even know and introduce myself as his daughter."

"Shoot, I knew I should have gone with you. If you want to, check into a motel and I'll meet you this evening. I can be there by five."

"No, I think I can do this. I just need a pep talk."

"All right then. Quit acting like a wimp. Get your butt down that driveway and act like Arnold Swartzenegger in *The Terminator*."

"I'll do it. Thanks, Godzilla."

"You're welcome, Arnold."

Maybe this is the miracle: good friends to pick you up when you fall.

Delta

The redwood cabin at the end of a winding driveway lined with loblolly pines features a large lake bordering the west side and a front porch stretching the length of the house and curving around both sides.

Carl Jordan is waiting for me on the porch. I'd know him anywhere. His hat is pushed back so he can see the driveway, a tall glass sits on the table beside his rocking chair and a walking cane leans against the table.

When he sees my car, he stands up, shrunken with age, at least three inches shorter than I remember. But his eyes are the same—the dark green of bottle glass—and his mouth has that same full bottom lip and heart-shaped upper. In spite of the weathered skin, he still has the sharply defined cheekbones and patrician nose of a handsome man.

I park in the shade and walk slowly toward him, wondering who will speak first and what we will say. My feet thunder on the wooden steps and my face is frozen, half smile, half uncertainty.

"You look like your mother."

His voice cracks, and I'm amazed to see tears leaking out of his eyes and settling into the creases of his sun-weathered face.

I could say, You look like somebody I used to know. Instead I sit stiff-backed on the rocking chair facing his, holding on to my purse and fighting the urge to run.

"I'm not going to pretend this is the televised reunion of some long-lost father and his daughter. I just want to know why you left."

"Because I am a coward."

We size each other up while the word echoes between us.

"If you're trying to justify yourself, it didn't work."

"This probably won't make any sense to you, but your mother was beautiful and perfect and far too good for the likes of me."

"Don't you dare blame this on my mother."

This reunion is rapidly disintegrating. I stand up, intending to leave before I explode. But the thought of Antonio waiting in Clarksdale plops me back into the chair.

"Every day I'd wake up thinking, *Today is the day*

she leaves me. And then one day it got so bad I figured I'd be the one to leave. I figured she'd find somebody who deserved her, somebody who could give both of you the life I never could have."

Okay, so this is where I got my running gene. My anger dies in a wave of empathy.

"And in all these years you never wanted to find us? Never wanted to know how we were doing or what we looked like or whether we needed you?"

"Wait here."

His rocking chair creaks when he hobbles into the house leaning heavily on his cane. I think about the years and how all of us weave them into blankets that tell our stories. When life gets cold and scary and threatening, some of us can use these blankets to keep ourselves safe and warm, but others use them merely as places to hide.

The tree frogs are starting their evening song and from the lake a giant bullfrog chimes in. Soon it will be night and I'll either go to a motel room alone, or I'll patch that big hole in my blanket left by Daddy's absence and invite him to visit me in Tupelo.

The screen door pops open and Daddy comes

out with a bulky scrapbook held together with rubber bands.

"I kept this," he says.

When he opens the book, yellowed newspaper articles spill across the pages: me in a cap and gown receiving the Balfour Award, me signing copies of my first travel guide, my two wedding announcements, Em and me at her Christmas benefit for the animal shelter, my mother's obituary.

He stuck the clippings to the page with old-fashioned glue that over the years created big discolored patches. The edges of the album are torn, some of the pages pulled loose from the binder and falling out.

I can picture Daddy sitting alone poring over this evidence of a family he barely knew, wondering if he made the right choice, wondering what would happen if he waltzed back into their lives.

Everything he's feeling shows in his face. I don't have to ask the questions to know that running away has haunted Carl Jordan his entire life.

And I don't have to ponder my own motives before I realize that the road stops here. I can't run anymore.

In this crude rocking chair on this rustic front porch in this stranger's house, my past and my future have collided. If I'm ever to live without the burning urge to put on my pink high-top running shoes and forget everything, this place is where I start.

"Daddy, I have a small apartment in Tupelo. I'd like you to go home with me."

"For how long?"

"As long as it takes to really find each other again."

"Yes, I will."

The look he gives me is filled with a thousand regrets tinged with a thousand pieces of hope.

CHAPTER 20

Appreciating the natural beauty of the Black
Hills is much like appreciating your past.
The Seasoned Traveler's Guide to
South Dakota,
Delta Jordan

Delta

It's late when I leave Daddy to pack for tomorrow's
trip home. I check into the Ramada Inn in Columbus
then call to tell Em the news. This is an easy conversation. I know her so well I can write a script for
her beforehand and get it almost word-for-word.

The harder call is to tell Antonio I won't be re-
turning to Clarksdale. When he answers I don't
beat around the bush.

"I've found Daddy and I'm bringing him home."

"This is wonderful news."

"Back to Tupelo, Antonio. Not Clarksdale."

"Delta, that's as it should be. Spend time with your father, get to know him again. I'm not going anywhere. And when the time is right, I'll get to know him, too."

My Lord, did I scratch an artist and find a prince? Every cliché I've imagined myself to be flies out the window. I should write a new kind of guide, tell women everywhere to travel abroad, be brave, be open to new experiences, don't worry about frivolous things such as different countries, different cultures and age barriers.

With the right person, none of that matters.

"Delta, are you there?"

"Yes, I'm here."

"I am there with you, beautiful lady, holding your hand."

"Thank you, Antonio."

It's easy for him to say that on the telephone. I hope he'll still feel the same way after he sees Carl Jordan. Look what happened after I met his mother.

Oh, Lord.

I call Em again. "What have I gotten myself into? Bringing Daddy home could ruin everything."

"The Uncle Carl I remember is not like Gina Donacelli. I don't picture him sticking his head in the oven."

"No, I don't think he is, but what am I going to do with him, though? Lord, Em. I never thought of that. My apartment's barely big enough for Antonio and me, let alone a third person."

"Delta, maybe it's time for you to get a house. Or two houses. Side by side. One for you and one for Uncle Carl."

A twenty-year mortgage means settling into one place, my name on a deed, permanence.

And then there's Italy.

"Delta, are you okay?"

"I think so. But you'd better get on your hotline to God just to make sure."

I don't know why I feel better after I talk to Em, but I do. It has always been this way, Em doing my spiritual work and me handling her practical problems.

I think it's high time for both of us to branch out

and become multidimensional women. Maybe we already have, and all we need is to take the next step to find out.

"I'm going to plant sunflower seeds when I get home," Em told me on the plane coming home. "Next summer we'll have our own sunflower fields."

It's a beautiful image to cling to: Em and me dancing in the sunflower fields, arms and minds wide open, ready to embrace every possibility.

Emily

The first thing that hits me when I wake up is that I am alone in this bed. The reality of not having Mike is as fresh and sharp as it was almost a year ago. The difference is that this reality is no longer an unbearable pain but a sweet remembering that will always flow through my blood and be carved in my bones.

As long as we have memory, nothing is ever lost. And even if memory fades, I believe the people we hold close to our hearts will make themselves known in the whisper of spring rains against the windowpane, the brilliance of yellow sunflowers in a summer field, the sigh of fall winds against the cheek, the glow of a single star on a cold December night.

I toss back the covers and go to retrieve my mail, then stand barefoot in the chill of October and rip into a letter from Women's Hospital in Tupelo.

Dear Mrs. Jones,
Thank you for the lovely blankets. Currently we have two premature, motherless babies who have been left in our care, and we are very grateful that someone loved them enough to help keep them warm.
Sincerely,
Janice Blankenship
Pediatric Administrator

I'd turn a cartwheel if I wouldn't break bones, but I'm light years removed from my cheerleader days so I content myself with a Texas *yippee!* then dance inside for coffee. Taking it on the deck so I can watch the eagles, I connect with this tranquil place before I start calling the women in my church who knit and sew.

Laura McCord is the first on my list. I explain the Linus Project to her, then ask if she'd like to become a charter member in the new chapter I'm forming.

"Well, goodness, yes. I'll bring lemon icebox pie."

All of a sudden I see the lemon pie metamorphosing from a symbol of the sick and afflicted into a symbol of hope. Yes, I tell her.

Then I call the rest of the women on my list and tap into my hotline with prayers of thanks and a small petition for Delta and Uncle Carl.

They're arriving in Tupelo today, and all I ask is that they will find the mercy of forgiveness and the grace of love.

After I finish my calls, I go back inside to dress. I'm heading to Wal-Mart in Fulton to pick up plenty of yarn for tonight's charter meeting of the Linus Project at my warehouse.

Before I head out the door the phone rings.

"Hey there." Cliff's voice booms with good cheer. This is one of the things I like about him; no matter how aggravated he gets, he rebounds quickly and falls into his usual, jocular mood.

"Hey there, yourself. What's up?"

"I'd like to come to Tupelo. Spend a couple of nights at your house."

"Not yet, Cliff. I'm not ready to take Smith Lake into my house."

"Okay. Take your time. I'm coming over this Saturday to visit my sister, anyhow. Maybe we can have dinner, take in a movie."

"Or watch TV here. I like quiet, cozy evenings, if that's not too boring for you."

"I like quiet and cozy almost as much as I do all the rest of it."

A month ago I would have panicked trying to figure out *all the rest of it*. Now I say "Good," then walk out the door with my purse on my arm and nothing but yarn on my mind. When I see an eagle from the corner of my eye, I don't even wonder what the flutter of wings is trying to tell me. I already know. *Fly*, they're saying, and I'm trying to give it my best effort.

Delta

"I don't want to be a burden to you."

My father is standing in the middle of my small

living room while I'm trying to figure out whether I should sleep on the sofa and give him the bedroom or just the reverse. Of course, the biggest thing I'm trying to figure out is whether he'll stay for the rest of my life and what to do with him if he does.

I guess neither of us thought this through. But he's here now, frail and uncertain-looking in his Mississippi State baseball jacket and his ancient felt fedora with the sweat-stained band.

"All I know to do is take this one day at a time."

I say this with my usual display of efficiency and confidence, then I realize that all my life I've been living from one day to the next, suitcase at the ready, minimal possessions, my mental gears set to Run.

"Sit down, please."

He removes his hat and sits stiffly in a wingback chair while I take the sofa.

"Daddy, do you want merely to get to know me and then leave again and go on about your business, or do you want to become part of my life? I have to know."

"I'd like to stay. All these years I've been trying to come home again, inching my way north, but when I got to Columbus I stopped. I don't know.

Maybe I convinced myself you wouldn't want to see me or maybe I was just scared there was no such thing as second chances."

"I'm scared, too. About second chances. Let me get us something to drink. Coffee?"

He tells me, "Yes, with cream and sugar," and I file this tidbit away as the first personal knowledge I have had about my daddy since I was six. When I return with two cups of coffee I tell him about Antonio and I don't leave out a single detail, including the fact that I'm scared to let myself love him.

Our silence fills the room, a proverbial elephant tripping over furniture and knocking over lamps and crashing through the floor, while Carl Jordan tries to figure out how to be a father again and I try to figure out how to be a daughter.

Finally he says, "I want to meet him," and I see the rightness of this.

No tiptoeing around the truth. Get everything out in the open, find out if it works, and if it doesn't, figure out a way to fix it.

"All right. We'll go to Clarksdale. I'll book a room

for you. But, Daddy, you should know I'll be staying with him in Clarksdale and wherever we go next."

"I wouldn't have it any other way. Listen, I'm not destitute. I may look like a railroad bum, but I've lived frugally and over the years I've managed to save a fair amount. After I meet this young man of yours, I may buy a little house close to you. I might get a parrot."

"A parrot?"

"I had one when I was down in the Florida Keys. He cussed like a sailor. I'm going to train this one to say, 'You lucky dog.'"

I walk down the street with my daddy to have barbecue at Jim's, and by the time we get back home, he's ready for a nap. While he's sleeping, I call Antonio.

"Daddy and I will be heading your way tomorrow. He's the only family I have and I want you to know him."

"I'll look forward to that."

"And Antonio, there's something else I want you to know."

"What is that, beautiful lady?"

Everything about me tightens: my hands, my chest, my throat. Then I take a big breath and release the words that have been locked inside me for years.

"That I love you."

"I love you, too, Delta. And I will forever."

I don't need a parrot to tell me I'm lucky. Every morning I will wake up to this knowledge, and when I go to bed at night the last thing I will say is thank you.

True appreciation of a place requires an understanding of its history as well as an acknowledgment of its unique beauty. The same is true of families. As you enjoy the Paleolithic and Neolithic history of Umbria, be still and learn to love your own history and the myriad, remarkable individuals who helped shape you.

The Seasoned Traveler's Guide to Umbria,
Delta Jordan

Emily

Although she has the longest way to come, Lucille is the first to arrive for my Thanksgiving supper. I think she puts Geritol in her coffee.

In spite of her age and the ten-hour drive, she swaggers through the front door and bear-hugs me while Leo races to my bedroom and hides.

"You're getting skinny."

"Thanks."

"I didn't mean that as a compliment." She marches down the hall, tosses her bag into the bedroom Delta used, then comes back and props her boots on my coffee table. "Where is everybody and why don't I smell turkey cooking?"

"They'll be along shortly and we're not having turkey this year."

"Why didn't you tell me you didn't want to cook? I'd have stuffed a bird last night and brought it up from Texas."

"Remember when I said I'm starting some new traditions? Well, this year I'm serving pork tenderloin, and I've changed the guest list. Let me get us some eggnog."

"I thought that was for Christmas."

I'm hoping it's for anesthesia. I pour her an extra large cup then sit on the sofa beside her.

"You've invited that Booth fellow, haven't you?"

"Yes, I have. He's an old friend and a good companion and I don't know if he'll ever be part of this family legally, but that's my decision."

"You think I'm fixing to make a fool of myself, don't you?"

"I don't know. Are you?"

She drinks the whole cup then gets up and pours herself another.

"All I have to say is this. If he ever mistreats you I'll horsewhip his butt all the way to Texas and back."

"Thank you, Lucille."

"Horsefeathers. You're my family. What would an outrageous old coot like me do by myself if I get so mean I run everybody off?" She takes another sip of eggnog then gives me that straightforward look she's famous for. "I'm not mean, am I?"

"Not yet. I'll let you know if you get too close."

"By the way, where's Delta?"

"In Italy. With Antonio."

"Has the lovebug bit everybody? Next thing you know I'll be chasing my old buffalo turd of a foreman around the ranch."

My doorbell rings and in walks Buddy Earl and

Doris Watson, dressed in plaid Bermudas in deference to this unseasonably mild day, and both wearing cowboy hats. Wait till I tell Delta.

"Buddy Earl, have you landed a woman?" Lucille says.

I wink at my neighbor and his constant companion to show she means no harm. After I make the introductions she says, "Who's going to show up next? The President? I'll swear, Emily, if you don't beat all."

"I'll take that as a compliment, Lucille."

She's too busy asking Buddy Earl about his Stetson to respond. Michele and Davis arrive next, along with Aunt Gertrude and Uncle Simpson, then Brennan, Janice and the boys, followed by Laura and Jim McCord.

My house is filled with people and excitement and good things to eat. A miracle, really, considering everything. I know holidays are supposed to be the hardest, but I think that's only if you try to keep them exactly as they were—the same people, the same food, the same china. That kind of slavery to tradition turns the empty chair at the table into a screaming reminder of loss.

Look at me now, I tell Mike. Something catches my eye and I turn toward the window just in time to see a pair of powerful wings gliding on the downdraft as an eagle lands atop the bald cypress.

Laura hands me two lemon icebox pies, then follows me to the serving bar.

"I hope it's all right," she says. "I didn't ask."

"You don't have to. I now call these celebration pies. Maybe you ought to make something else for the sick and afflicted."

"I started last week when the preacher's wife got a bad cold. Wheat bread." She glances around. "Can I help you with anything, Emily?"

"Help me pass around the eggnog."

If that lantern jaw silhouetted through my glass door is any sign, Cliff Booth just charged up on his white horse. Translated, flashy white Porsche.

"Keep it low-key," I whisper, and he winks at me.

Meaning what? He will or he won't?

"You remember Cliff Booth," I say to my family, then keep a sharp eye on the door while I make the rest of the introductions.

The doorbell pings, announcing my last guest.

Uncle Carl is wearing a wool suit, vintage 1960s, and he's sweating with heat and nerves. I hug him and say, "Everything is going to be all right."

And it really is. Finally I know this is true. I live in a world where a long-lost father can be welcomed back into the family, a scared woman can hang up her running shoes and follow her heart instead of the road, and a widow coming undone can put herself back together in a new and improved version of her old frivolous, shallow self.

While Cliff plays guardian angel at Uncle Carl's side, Lucille demands more eggnog and Aunt Gertrude wonders why she couldn't go to Disneyland, aka Italy, with Delta, I carve the pork loin.

If Delta's phone calls are any indication, we'll all be going to Italy soon. For a wedding.

I picture myself in charge, leading Uncle Carl through the labyrinth of international travel like a pro, my gifts for Rosa piled high on the smart cart I'm pulling, no Franciscan priests damaged in the process. I see my children and Lucille awestruck with admiration that the woman who once cried because she didn't want to get on a plane is no longer afraid to fly.

The real miracle, though, is that even without a plane, I know how to fly.

*Be sure to return to NEXT in March for more
entertaining women's fiction for every woman
who has wondered, "What's next?" in her life.
For a sneak preview of Connie Lane's
KNIT TWO TOGETHER,
coming to NEXT in March,
please turn the page.*

"You gonna go inside, or you just gonna stand here and stare?" Her daughter's voice snapped Libby back to reality.

Libby tossed the key into the air and caught it. "Gonna go inside," she said, and then unlocked the front door. She paused on the threshold, drew in a breath for courage. And immediately gagged.

"I think something's dead in there," she said at the same time Meghan squealed.

She wasn't going to let that stop her. She hadn't come hundreds of miles to be chased away by a smell.

There was a wooden chair on the front porch and Libby propped it against the door to keep it open and allow some air inside.

As ready as she'd ever be, she stepped into Barb's Knits.

"The place is a dump." Meghan was right behind her and as always, her daughter had a way of distilling a situation to its essence.

Barb's Knits was, indeed, a dump.

The room they stepped into must have once been the living room of the first-floor apartment. In addition to a dust-covered counter and cash register on the left, there was a wall of shelves and books directly ahead of them, and across from it, tables where tape measures, scissors and other supplies were piled. Beyond a doorway was another room and from what Libby could see, another past that. She peered through the gloom. There was lots of yarn everywhere, lots of dust, and—Libby shivered—even some mouse droppings.

And something else.

In spite of Meghan's half-heard warnings about ghosts, ax murderers and creepy crawlers, Libby started into the next room without hesitation, her attention caught by a display table.

The table had two tiers. The bottom one was stacked with wool, but Libby hardly noticed. Her eyes were on the teddy bear on the top tier. A cocoa colored bear with one missing eye.

"Mom, you okay?"

"Of course," Libby answered automatically, even though she wasn't sure she was. Though she had no clear memory of the bear, there was something vaguely familiar about it. He was dressed in a knit fisherman's sweater, handmade by the looks of it, and the fur on his right arm was nearly gone, as if years of hugs had worn it away. Instinctively, Libby touched the bear with one finger, then stepped back. She swore he was watching her with that one good eye of his.

"Mom!" Meghan's voice called from the front room. "You're awfully quiet in there. Did you get kidnapped?"

"I'm just looking around," she told Meghan. "That's all."

"Yeah, right. And I just fell off a turnip truck," she said as she entered the room.

It was what Libby always said when Meghan tried to pull a fast one on her, and Libby smiled grimly.

"Come on. We're leaving." Libby swept past her daughter and toward the front door.

"But, Mom!" Meghan dropped the bear she'd picked up and shuffled behind. "We just got here and it's not like I want to stay or anything but, gee, why did you get all nutso about the bear?"

No sooner was Meghan out on the porch than Libby closed the front door and locked it. It wasn't until she pocketed the key and turned to walk down the stairs that she realized there were tears in Meghan's eyes.

Libby's heart broke. She reached for her daughter's hand. "I'm sorry, honey. I didn't mean to take it out on you. Maybe you were right and I was wrong. Maybe it was a mistake to come here after all." She took a deep breath. "I thought…"

"I know." Meghan gave her hand a squeeze. "I mean, I think I get it. Sort of. You thought you wouldn't care."

As insights went, it was so obvious Libby wondered why she'd never thought of it herself. "I just didn't expect—"

"The bear, yeah. So what's the story?"

Libby had never lied to Meghan about her past. Oh, she didn't know the whole truth. That would be too much of a burden for any child her age. But when Meghan asked questions about Libby's childhood and about why Libby had been raised by the Palmers, her father's parents, Libby had never hesitated to give her as much of the story as would satisfy her. As much as she could handle.

She wasn't about to start playing with the truth now.

"I'm not sure about the bear," Libby told her daughter. "Not exactly, anyway. But there's something about him that makes me feel as if I've seen him before." A touch like cold fingers skittered over her shoulders and Libby shivered. "I don't know," she said. "I know it sounds weird, but I think maybe he used to be mine."

The best things in life are free

Kate Bishop needs money and fast.
Her roof needs replacing. Her kids need
tuition and her ex-husband is a cheap creep.
Then her wildest fantasy comes true—
she wins the lottery. Suddenly, everything
changes. Her wish came true, but now what?

Wish Come True

USA TODAY bestselling author
Patricia Kay

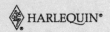

EVERLASTING LOVE™

Every great love has a story to tell™

Save $1.⁰⁰ off

the purchase of any Harlequin Everlasting Love novel

Coupon valid from January 1, 2007 until April 30, 2007.

Valid at retail outlets in the U.S. only.
Limit one coupon per customer.

5 65373 00076 2   (8100)0 11302

HEUSCPN0407

EVERLASTING LOVE™

Every great love has a story to tell™

Fall from Grace

Kristi Gold

Save $1.⁰⁰ off

the purchase of
any Harlequin
Everlasting Love novel

Coupon valid from January 1, 2007
until April 30, 2007.

Valid at retail outlets in Canada only.
Limit one coupon per customer.

52607370

HECDNCPN0407

Millionaire of the Month
Bound by the terms of a will,
six wealthy bachelors discover
the ultimate inheritance.

USA TODAY bestselling author
MAUREEN CHILD

Millionaire of the Month: Nathan Barrister
Source of Fortune: Hotel empire
Dominant Personality Trait: Gets what he wants

THIRTY DAY AFFAIR
SD #1785 Available in March

When Nathan Barrister arrives at the Lake Tahoe
lodge, all he can think about is how soon he can
leave. His one-month commitment feels like solitary
confinement—until a snowstorm traps him with lovely
Keira Sanders. Suddenly a thirty-day affair sounds like
just the thing to pass the time…

In April,
#1791 HIS FORBIDDEN FIANCÉE, Christie Ridgway

In May,
#1797 BOUND BY THE BABY, Susan Crosby

Romantic
SUSPENSE

Excitement, danger and passion guaranteed!

Same great authors and riveting editorial
you've come to know and love
from Silhouette Intimate Moments.

New York Times
bestselling author
Beverly Barton
is back with the
latest installment
in her popular
miniseries,
The Protectors.
HIS ONLY
OBSESSION
is available
next month from
Silhouette®
Romantic Suspense

Look for it wherever you buy books!

REQUEST YOUR FREE BOOKS!

2 FREE NOVELS PLUS 2 FREE GIFTS!

There's the life you planned. And there's what comes next.

NEXT07R